W9-BCO-246

Horse Mad
Heights

6 Horse Mad

Kathy Helidoniotis

WALRUS
B O O K S

Copyright © Kathy Helidoniotis 2009.

Walrus Books, an imprint of Whitecap Books

All rights reserved. No part of this publication may be reproduced, stored in a retrieval system, or transmitted in any form or by any means, electronic, mechanical, photocopying, recording, or otherwise, without the prior written permission of the publisher.

This edition published in North America in 2010 by Whitecap Books Ltd. For more information, contact Whitecap Books, 351 Lynn Avenue, North Vancouver, British Columbia, Canada V7J 2C4. Visit our website at www.whitecap.ca.

First published in English in Sydney, Australia by HarperCollins Publishers Australia Pty Limited in 2009. This edition is published by arrangement with HarperCollins Publishers Australia Pty Limited.

The author has asserted their right to be identified as the author of this work.

Library and Archives Canada Cataloguing in Publication

Helidoniotis, Kathy
    Horse mad heights / Kathy Helidoniotis.

(Horse mad)
ISBN 978-1-55285-997-1

        I. Title. II. Series: Helidoniotis, Kathy. Horse mad series.

PZ7.H374Hob 2010   j823'.92   C2009-906418-9

The publisher acknowledges the financial support of the Canada Council for the Arts, the British Columbia Arts Council, and the Government of Canada through the Canada Book Fund (CBF). Whitecap Books also acknowledges the financial support of the Province of British Columbia through the Book Publishing Tax Credit.

Canada Council   Conseil des Arts
for the Arts   du Canada

BRITISH COLUMBIA
ARTS COUNCIL

Printed in Canada.

10 11 12 13 14   5 4 3 2 1

For Mariana, John, Simon,
Jamie and Monique
with all my love,
and for Seb
with all my heart.

Happy 9th Birthday
Brookie
Love
Nana

G'day mate!

This story takes place in Australia — so if you want to brush up on your Aussie slang (what are 'joddies'?), just flip to the helpful glossary at the back of the book!

one

Goodbye Shady Creek

'Do you really have to go?'

I glanced at Becky Cho, my best friend. She looked back at me with wide dark eyes, stroking the neck of her gorgeous bay part-Arab gelding, Charlie, while we rode together down our favourite trail.

There was so much I wanted to say, but I looked at my hands instead. Pretending that I'd forgotten how to correctly hold my Honey horse's reins was much easier than telling Becky my true feelings. I fidgeted, checking and re-checking that each rein was passing between my third and little fingers and across my palm and was locked between my index finger and thumb.

It wasn't that I didn't want to talk to her about it — I told Becky everything. It was just that explaining how much I would miss her and home, and how scared I was, was going to hurt and I'm not the world's biggest fan of pain. It had been hard enough getting used to being without Jenna, my best friend from the city, when we moved to Shady Creek. And it had been really hard being away from Becky for those four weeks at the Waratah Grove Riding Academy. But it was going to be impossible being without my friends at Linley Heights School.

But none of that came out of my mouth. 'Linley's a great school,' I said. 'I can't really turn this down.' I rubbed my fingers in my mare's honey-coloured mane.

Becky sighed. 'It's so gonna stink here without you. You get to come home for school holidays, don'tcha?'

'Course,' I said. 'And I get some weekends back home too. They call them exeat weekends. But Honey will only come home for the school holidays. Hey, d'you reckon the Three Creepketeers will miss me at Riding Club?'

Becky laughed. 'Like a hole in the head.'

'I thought they already had plenty of those,' I said, and winked.

'What about you?' I went on. 'You're going to Shady Creek and Districts High School. I can't believe I won't be there with you.'

'And I can't believe this is our last trail ride together. Until Easter, anyway.'

Becky snapped a low-hanging branch from a tree and used it as a fly swatter. It was hot. My second January in Shady Creek and I was no more used to it than I'd been a year ago.

'Tell me about it,' I said.

I was tempted to follow Becky's lead and take fly-control matters into my own hands. But knowing Honey like I did, I chose to put up with the flies. Anything but wave a stick around her head. My poor mare was still haunted by the cruel treatment she'd received from her previous owners. When I rubbed behind her ears I could still feel the scar that the whip had made. Just thinking of it made me shiver.

'Sure you won't need the float?' Becky was trying her best to sound cheerful. But I knew her too well to be fooled.

I shook my head. 'Linley are sending their horse truck. There's another girl going from somewhere around here so we're sharing the cost. Dad doesn't wanna float Honey that far anyway.'

'Said your goodbyes at Shady Trails?' Becky held her reins in her right hand, practising the Western neck-reining we'd learnt last year.

I nodded. 'Pree cried, Mrs McMurray cried, I cried. Even Sam cried.'

'*Sam*?' Becky stared at me, incredulous. I knew what she was thinking. Samantha was the best stable manager in the history of managed stables and had never seemed the waterworks kind. 'But she's so tough.'

'Maybe not,' I said.

'What about your job? Has Mrs Mac found a replacement yet?'

'Yep. But she promised I could work here every school holidays. I'll miss working with Pree, though. I'll miss Pree full stop.'

Priyanka Prasad, fellow Trailer and horsy joke-teller extraordinaire, had become one of my best friends. I didn't know how I was going to survive the next eleven weeks without her either.

'It's so cool Pree'll be in Year Seven with me,' Becky said. 'Won't be so scary with her around.'

I felt a pressure around my heart, like a giant pair of hands had squeezed it for just a moment. Was I jealous? I shook my head. 'Don't they have a high school in Pinebark Ridge?'

'Nuh. That's why it's called Shady Creek and Districts. The Ridge is one of the districts. Kids from all around come here.' Becky gave me a sly smile. 'If they don't go to fancy schools on riding scholarships like you, that is!'

'Ha ha. Feel like a trot?'

'You bet!'

Becky collected her reins and squeezed her calf muscles against Charlie's sides. The gelding responded immediately, as always. We fell into single file, Honey and me behind Charlie and Beck, and trotted down the trail.

'Wanna canter?' Becky called over her shoulder.

'What are you waiting for?' I yelled back.

Becky didn't wait for me to change my mind. Charlie stretched into a gentle canter and Honey, responding to my leg aids, cantered after him. I loved this so much. I never felt more alive than when I was riding. Honey's hooves beat along with my heart and the bush melted away like a green and grey blur. We were too fast for the flies to settle on our faces now. I felt fused with my horse. I felt that she and I were one being and we were flying. My tummy tumbled with exhilaration. I'd cantered before, too many times to count, but it was never anything less than joyful. Especially on a trail ride. Especially with my best friend.

Becky slowed Charlie to a trot, then a walk.

'Time to start cooling them down,' she said. 'They'll wanna eat as soon as they get home. If they're still too hot when they do, they could get colic.'

We walked our horses side by side in the direction of home. The sun was just beginning its descent. It shone through the gum leaves overhead, gilding them like precious jewels. My ears drank in the sounds of the bush. I knew I'd miss each one of them. The gentle swish of branches, the screeches of the cheeky white cockatoos and the parrots that were painted the colour of bush flowers, the step-stepping of horse's hooves on the baked grey track. I could smell the dirt and the heat and Honey and the trees. Twigs scratched at my arms and flies danced on my nose. This was riding in Shady Creek.

We emerged from the trail straight onto my street and walked the horses across the lawns and past Shady Creek Riding Club. Honey threw back her head and danced, then burst into a trot. She was eager to get home to the dinner of green and white chaff and horse pellets she knew was waiting for her (with a few carrots added for good measure).

'No, Honey!' I scolded, gathering my reins for extra control.

'That's a bad habit,' Becky said. 'One day she might take off on you. Back her up a few steps. Make her understand that she goes faster when she's told to, not when she wants to.'

I gathered my reins and pulled my hands against my tummy, sinking my seat into the saddle.

'Back, back!' I said.

Honey stepped backwards. When I was happy I released her mouth and urged her forward again. This time she got the message. We walked home.

'Good on you, Ash!' Becky gave me the thumbs up.

We pulled our horses up on my front lawn, Becky careful to hold Charlie's head away from the grass. She never let him snack when he was bridled.

We slid to the ground and faced one another.

Becky shrugged. 'I guess this is it.'

I winced. 'I've never wanted anyone to say that to me.'

'Will you miss me?' Becky gave me her cheekiest grin.

'Will I ever!' I wrapped my arms around her neck and held her close.

'I won't come and see you off tomorrow if that's okay,' Becky said once we'd broken apart. 'I stink at real goodbyes.'

'Me too.' I rubbed at my nose, knowing from the tight feeling in my throat and the burning in my eyes that I was about to cry.

'Don't start,' Becky moaned. 'You'll set me off.'

Tears streamed down my face and my nose started to run. I rubbed everything away with my hands and wiped them on my joddies.

'Real ladylike,' Becky said, her smile wobbling. 'Betcha no one at Linley does *that*.'

'I'll be one of a kind then, eh?' I sniffled and wrapped my arms around Becky once more.

'Yuck!' she shrieked. 'At least wash your hands before you do that!'

I laughed and cried all at once and that's when I felt it. All that horrible pain I'd been trying to hide from. My chest ached and my throat burned. I was going to miss her so much.

'Goodbye, Beck,' I whispered.

'Bye, Ash,' she said.

We broke apart and I squeezed her hands. She was crying too.

'I'll email,' I said. 'And I'll call and text. And you can get me anytime on that cellphone Mum got for me.'

Becky nodded and let go of my hands. She gathered her reins, placed her left foot in the stirrup and bounced into her saddle, settling lightly on Charlie's back. The gelding looked over his shoulder, seeming to smile when he saw his mistress just where he liked her to be.

'Good luck, Ash.'

I patted Charlie's neck. 'Good luck to you too.'

Becky gave me a quick, sad smile and squeezed her calves against Charlie's sides. He sprang into a trot and then a canter. I watched until they rounded the corner. Becky never looked back once.

'Don't forget me,' I said. 'Please don't forget me.'

I had this terrible feeling all of a sudden that I shouldn't go to Linley. It was too scary. I couldn't leave Becky alone at Riding Club with the dreaded Creeps. And what if I hated the school? What if I was the worst rider there and everybody laughed at me? What if Honey was picked on in the paddock?

What if Mum forgot to feed Toffee? What if Jason learned to walk and talk and got into my room and finally finished off my headless horse clock while I was away? It was all too awful.

Honey nudged my shoulder.

'Sorry,' I said, wiping my face on my sleeve. 'I almost forgot about you.'

I loosened the girth two notches and ran my stirrups up, tucking the leathers inside the stirrups themselves. It was important to reward Honey for her hard work on the trail and to make sure the stirrups didn't bang against her sides.

'Ready?' I said.

I pulled the reins over Honey's head and held them under her chin in my right hand, picking up the slack with my left. I led her down our driveway into her corral and secured the reins to one of the loops of yellow twine that hung from a post. Twine was the best way to tie a horse to a stable, float, corral or fence — anything. It broke easily if the horse spooked and bolted, and could save not only the horse but also expensive tack from harm.

I unbuckled the girth all the way and let it fall loose, ducking under Honey's neck to pick it up on her far side before throwing it over the saddle.

I stepped behind her, running my hand across her rump and talking to her as I went, lifted the saddle gently from her back and settled it down on a rail a few horse lengths away. Honey had never chewed on her saddle or knocked it down, but, from my experience with horses, there was a first time for everything and I never wanted there to be a first time for saddle destruction.

I removed the saddle blanket and threw it over the corral rail to air and dry. Honey's coat was wet and dark with sweat. I hosed her down, starting with her feet and legs and finally her back and neck, then I ran a sweat scraper over her, squeezing as much water as I could from her coat. I rubbed her down with an old towel that I'd left flapping on the rail and threw a light cotton rug over her. I'd give her a good groom once she was fed, watered and dry.

I usually fed Honey in the paddock, so I untied the twine and led her out of the corral and into her paddock. Toffee, my mad miniature pony, was chasing his tail under Honey's big old tree. He stopped when he saw her and whinnied loudly.

Honey whinnied in reply. I closed the paddock gate behind her and unbuckled her throatlash, pulling the headpiece of the bridle over her ears and letting her release the bit from her mouth at her own pace. Once the bit was free, I rubbed at her neck and ducked through the fence to go and prepare dinner for my two horses.

In the stable, I measured the horses' feed into their wide feed buckets. One dipper of green chaff and two of white for Toffee with a half-dipper of pony pellets, and two dippers of green chaff and three of white for Honey with a full dipper of pellets. I sliced some carrots into eighths and threw them on top of the feed, squeezed a few squirts of molasses on top for good measure, and sprayed the chaff with water to remove any traces of dust. I felt better now that I was busy. I hadn't thought of how much I'd miss Mum and Dad and Jason and Becky and Pree for a couple of minutes at least.

My horses knew what was coming and met me at the paddock gate, stamping and nickering.

'It's not like you guys are starved or anything,' I said, a bucket in each hand. 'Anyone'd think you hadn't eaten in a week!'

I gently pushed them aside and emptied their feed buckets into their separate feed bins, well apart. They were good paddock mates but I didn't want a fight over food.

Honey took a huge bite and chewed happily. Toffee buried his face in his bin and crunched on a carrot.

I wandered over to Honey's tree and sat on the ground, leaning up against it. I let my eyes drink everything in: the paddocks, the corral, the stable and barn and pool, the house, my bedroom window. Even Flea's place next door. I would miss it all so much.

two

Linley Heights School

'This place is unbelievable,' Dad said, staring in awe as he parked our car in the Linley Heights School visitors' area.

'So is what you said about renting out my room,' I whined. 'Just because we have a Bed and Breakfast doesn't mean it's okay to let just anyone sleep in my—'

'Okay, okay!' Dad said, holding up his hands. 'I was only stirring, you goose. As if I'd let anyone sleep in your room! They'd probably never make it out alive with all that horse junk you store in there. We'd be down a night's pay!'

'Funny,' I said, rolling my eyes. 'But don't give up your day job.'

'Already did!' Dad grinned and wiggled his eyebrows.

Dad had been extra happy since he'd decided to take a year off nursing to open Miller Lodge. It had been nice having him around more, and not having to tiptoe about because he was sleeping off the night shift. But I couldn't help worrying about money. I'd always taken care of most of Honey's and Toff's expenses myself with my Horse Cents fund. But now that I was only working school holidays at Shady Trails, I knew I'd have to rely on Mum and Dad to help me out. The price of feed was rising thanks to the Shady Creek clouds' stubborn refusal to squeeze out even one drop of rain in months and I was scared. What would happen to my horses if Miller Lodge didn't make any money? What would happen to us if Dad never went back to nursing and Mum decided to stay home with Jason rather than go back to plumbing (although after having changed a few of Jase's nappies I'd swear that plumbing was less stinky and involved much less sludge)? I didn't know. And I hated not knowing.

'Penny for your thoughts,' Dad said as he popped the car boot open.

'For ten bucks you can have every single one of 'em.' I held out my hand, hopeful.

Dad tousled my hair. 'Not a chance.'

I smoothed my hair frantically and wrenched down the sun visor so I could check my reflection in the mirror. A freckled face with darkish eyes and long dark, recently-tousled-and-therefore-unfit-to-venture-from-the-car hair looked back at me. 'Dad! I'm in *high school*. High school kids can't have bad hair!'

'Correction,' Dad said. 'You're almost in high school. According to my calculations you can have bad hair for at least the next three minutes.'

I got out of the car muttering under my breath in much the same way Mum does when she's having one of her 'I will never ever understand men!' moments, and slammed the door. Then it hit me. I was at Linley. I was actually here. I stood on the spot and stared. And stared and stared.

I was standing in front of a huge, old sandstone building that looked more like a castle than a school. I could see that it was built like a rectangle with a hollow space in the middle. And it had turrets! I squinted up at them, expecting a knight to suddenly appear at a window and shoot an arrow at me or something. There was a vast green lawn with a rope fence around it and flowerbeds bursting with colour. On either side of the main building were playing fields. There were other buildings behind, but I couldn't make them out from where I was standing. I craned my neck. Where were the paddocks? Where were the horses and stables? Where was Honey?

'This looks just like my old university,' Dad said. 'I hope you work harder here than I did at uni, though.'

'How do we get in?' I said, almost speechless.

Dad pointed to enormous double wooden doors. Girls of all shapes and sizes were streaming through them with their parents and suitcases in tow. Some were shrieking and hugging each other. Some were hugging their parents. Some were rolling their eyes and picking at their fingernails.

'Only the boarders start today. Gives you guys a chance to settle in.' Dad opened the boot and hauled out one of my two suitcases. 'What've you got in here? Rocks?'

I shook my head. 'Books. *Practical Horse Care, Stable Management, The Horse at Grass, The Complete Dictionary of Equ—*'

Dad threw up his hands. 'Spare me the Complete Dictionary of Anything Equine! Isn't it bad enough I have to live with a walking horse encyclopaedia?'

'Work on your jokes while I'm away, okay?' I said, grinning. Dad's jokes were pretty bad, but I knew I'd miss them anyway.

Dad waggled his eyebrows again and pulled the other suitcase and some smaller bags from the boot. I opened the back passenger door and grabbed my pillow and saddle carry bag.

'Couldn't you have chucked that in the Linley truck?' Dad said.

I sucked in my breath and held the back of my hand against my forehead. '*Chuck* my saddle? Perish the thought!'

Dad closed the boot and the doors and surveyed my mountain of belongings. 'I think it would've been easier to just drive the car into your room.'

I slung my saddle carry bag over my shoulder (thank goodness synthetic saddles are so light!) and grabbed another two bags. 'If only Mum could've come. She's got muscles like a racehorse.'

'It's all those dunnies she carries around,' Dad said, scooping up the rest of my things. 'But you know Jase doesn't travel so well. Mum had to stay home with him.'

I sighed, remembering the time we'd driven into town and Jason had been so carsick he'd made the eruption of Krakatoa look like a backyard fountain during water restrictions.

We joined the mass of girls and their parent-porters heading towards the double doors. I scanned the crowd. Would any of these girls be my friends?

The doors were huge. Everything about Linley so far was huge. Inside the doors was a vestibule with humungous glass cabinets on either side crammed full of trophies, plates, medals and black-and-white photos of girls in hats and gloves. The ceiling was high, really high. So high I felt like the smallest being on earth. I looked up until my neck started to ache.

'Wake up, Ash!' Dad said. His voice bounced around the vestibule. Some of the girls giggled.

'What?' I said. 'What did I do wrong?'

'We have to go over there.' Dad jerked his head to the left where another set of towering double doors opened onto an assembly hall. The hall was buzzing with activity. Parents and girls gathered around a series of tables set out in a horseshoe shape.

There was chatter and the scraping of chair legs and suitcases on the polished timber floor.

'C'mon, Ash,' Dad groaned, hauling my suitcases in the direction of one of the tables. Two happy-looking students in the light blue Linley tunic and dark navy panama hat I'd tried on during the holidays were sitting behind the table. A laminated sign attached to it said: *M–R*. 'M, that's us.'

We shuffled through the crowd and stopped in front of the table. The girls smiled.

'Name?' the taller one said.

Dad looked at me.

'Miller,' I said. 'Ashleigh Louise.'

The smaller girl flicked through some papers while the other peeled a white sticky label from a sheet. My name was typed on it in neat black letters. She handed it to me. I stuck it on my chest and patted it down.

'Room Two-Eleven-Two.'

'Huh?' I said.

The taller girl smiled. 'Two, that's floor two. Eleven is your room number and the last "two" is your bed number.'

'Here's a goodie bag,' Smaller Girl said, handing me a blue linen bag with the Linley crest emblazoned on both sides in white. I peered at her sticky label. Her name was Catherine. 'There's a school directory, the Linley prospectus and a copy of the *Linley Gazette* inside.'

'Where are the stables?' I asked.

I couldn't wait any longer. I had to know where Honey was and if she was okay. Had she been fed? Was her rug on right? Were her shoes secure? Was she lonely? Had she settled into her new home or was she afraid?

'Rider, eh?' Taller Girl said. I nodded. 'Me too. School tours leave every half-hour from the front lawn.'

'Put your things away first and join a tour group,' Catherine said. 'And there'll be a welcoming assembly in an hour and a half followed by lunch in the dining hall.' She beamed at us.

'Lunch?' Dad said hopefully. 'Sounds great.'

'How can you think of eating at a time like this?' I moaned, dragging at his arm.

'At a time like what?' he said, blank-faced.

'We need to find my room, dump my stuff and get to the stables. Fast!'

Dad rolled his eyes. 'Eleven weeks of almost horseless peace and quiet. I can't wait.'

He stooped to pick up my suitcases and ooofed loudly. Several girls turned to stare for a moment then returned to their conversations. I hoped they weren't talking about me.

'Let's go,' I nagged. 'Those cases shouldn't be a problem for you. Your new career is carrying suitcases up and down stairs, remember?'

Dad glowered. 'Why do I get the feeling you're still not entirely supportive of my decision to take a year off nursing, Ash?'

'Not now,' I said, then plunged into the crowd in what I hoped was the direction of the boarding house.

Thirteen minutes later (which could have been five had Dad listened to me and asked for directions) I held the doorknob of my assigned room in my hand. This was it — my home for the next eleven weeks. For the next year, actually. Who knew? Maybe it would be my home away from home for the next six years. It was impossible to say. One thing I did know for sure. Whoever was behind this door could make my life at Linley amazing or miserable. I twisted the doorknob slowly.

three

Roommates

'Who's there?' came a voice from inside.

I cleared my throat. 'It's Ashleigh. I guess I'm your roommate.' I looked over my shoulder at Dad, who gave me the thumbs up but said nothing. He knew I had to do this on my own.

I took a step inside the room. The first thing I saw was a huge window that seemed to overlook some sort of lawn. Under the window were two identical desks. The desk on the right had a series of school-type items — tubs of pens, a few thick books and a clock — arranged in neat order, tallest to smallest. It was sparkling clean. The desk on the left was clear. I assumed it was mine. Next to the desk was a single bed. It was made with crisp, pale blue sheets and a light blue, very snug-looking woollen blanket. I noticed the Linley crest on the blanket and smiled. There was a pillow too, but I wouldn't be needing that. I'd brought my own pillow from home and couldn't imagine how I'd get to sleep on anything else. I'd used a strange pillow at Waratah Grove, no worries, but Waratah Grove was only for four weeks. And I'd had my two incredible friends Tash Symon and Molly Bryant to pick me up when I was down. I had nobody at Linley. Not yet, anyway.

There was a strange smell. I took a deep whiff and wrinkled my nose.

'What's that stink?' I said, coughing.

A muffled squirting sound came from the right side of the room.

'What was that?' I took a step towards the noise.

A smallish girl with round eyes and dark bushy hair that hung around her face sat on the bed. She had a book open on her lap and was holding a gold spray can in her hand. 'It's my germ spray,' she croaked. She cleared her throat and held tight to her can.

'You spray germs around the room?'

The girl gasped. 'Definitely not! My spray kills all germs on contact.'

I held out my hand. 'I'm Ashleigh.'

She looked at my hand but didn't touch it. 'I heard you before.'

I examined my hand. 'Want to give it a spray?'

The girl beamed and ripped the lid from the can. 'Would you mind?'

I laughed, folding my arms so my hands were out of the firing line. 'I would, actually. What's your name?'

She snapped the lid back onto the can and sighed. 'Claire. Claire Carlson.'

I stepped closer. 'Nice to meet you. I hope you don't disinfect the horses with that stuff.'

Claire went pale. 'Horses? I never go anywhere near the dirty things. My parents have been writing to the principal since last year demanding that the riding program be discontinued. It's filthy having people touching those animals then using the facilities without even washing their hands.' She snapped the lid from the can again and squirted some spray into the air in a rainbow shape, delivering most of the squirts in my direction. Once she'd killed a few more germs she regained some colour. 'My parents are very active within the Parents' Association. Mum's president this year. She's promised to make horses history at Linley Heights.'

I stared at her, trying to work out if she was serious or pulling my leg. I'd made up my mind that I was going to be friends with everyone at Linley. But how could I be friends with someone who hated the one thing in life I was most passionate about? Jenna, my best friend from the city, had never exactly loved horses. Okay, so she'd never even liked them. But she'd always supported my riding, had helped me start up my Horse Cents fund, and had even had riding lessons just to please me. Claire was a whole new sack of chaff altogether.

'I certainly hope you're not one of these *riding* people,' she went on. 'I won't have filth in my room. I just won't have it.'

'Dad, it's okay to bring in my saddle now!' I hollered.

Claire gasped again and waved her hand frantically in front of her nose. 'A *saddle*! You can't have a saddle in here! This room has been thoroughly cleaned. Horses sweat on saddles!'

Dad burst into the room and collapsed on the empty bed, my saddle, snug in its saddle carry bag, slung over his arm. 'This your bed? Sure hope so! Gidday, love, I'm Ash's dad.' Dad smiled warmly at Claire who practically recoiled. 'Okay to just leave this here, is it? Although I'll bet you're one of those sensible types who stores her tack in the tack room like everybody else. Not like this one.' Dad jerked his head in my direction. 'No matter what we said, her mother and I couldn't convince her. Positive something terrible would happen to her saddle unless she slept with it under her pillow!'

Dad laughed at his own dumb joke and set my saddle on the floor, leaning it against the wall. I buried my face in my hands. I was finished at Linley before I'd even begun. My social life was finished anyway. All Claire Carlson had to do was tell one person, just one person, and the fact that Ashleigh Miller had the most embarrassing dad in the entire galaxy would spread around Linley like sawdust around a stable on a windy day.

'Dad,' I groaned, 'shouldn't we join a school tour?'

But Dad wasn't listening. He was too busy watching Claire turn an odd shade of grey. 'Saddle ... room ... my ... here ... in ... not,' she spluttered. 'Filth ... brutes ...'

'Are you all right?' Dad asked. His instincts were getting the better of him. I knew it! There was still a nurse in there somewhere. A fully employed, paid nurse!

Claire leaned under her bed, pulled out a vacuum cleaner and started cleaning the floor near my saddle.

Dad was spellbound. 'This is great, Ash. One term here and you'll be domesticated! Do you all get a vacuum cleaner?'

'Let's go find out,' I muttered, tugging on his sleeve.

Claire ripped the lid from her can and squirted at us as we left the room. As the door closed behind us I thought I heard her say something about house mistresses.

'She's really something, eh?' Dad said cheerfully. 'Just what you need — a nice new friend who'll set you a top example. By the time you get home on exeat you might actually be of some use to us in the B and B.'

'She's, um, interesting,' I said.

I couldn't imagine how I was going to share a room with Claire Carlson for even one night. We were totally incompatible. My heart ached for Becky. And for Jenna and Pree. My three best mates in the world. What I needed right now was to see Honey. I needed to bury my face in her neck and breathe in her horsiness. She would make everything all right. It was the one thing I was sure of.

four

Oh Honey,
Where Art Thou?

We made our way back down the stairs and out to the front lawn. It was so green and soft — like walking on a sheet of velvet. Mum would've been impressed. I don't think there was even one weed or bindi-eye in sight! Honey would love to graze here but somehow I didn't think horses would be welcome in this part of Linley Heights.

A crowd was gathered around a senior girl. Her uniform was different to the light blue tunic I'd seen so far. She was wearing a white cotton blouse with round collars (someone told me later it was a 'Peter Pan' collar) and a dark blue pleated skirt with very fine white pinstripes running through the fabric. She had on a matching blazer and a dark blue panama hat. I was fascinated by the yellow and white writing on the left-hand side of her blazer and squinted to read the words: *Debating Team, ISA Swimming, Polocrosse Captain.*

Hang on a moment — polocrosse captain!

I was instantly interested in knowing her better. A *lot* better. As the Year Seven riding scholarship student I was expected to be on the Linley polocrosse team, but I'd never played the game. I'd never even seen a match. I was dying to learn more.

'Welcome to Linley Heights School,' the girl said. Silence fell over the crowd. I smiled at a girl who looked a little like Becky, except her straight shiny black hair fell only to her shoulders and was cut into a short fringe in front. She had cute round glasses and wore a chain around her neck with a gold letter 'E' hanging from it. She smiled back.

The senior girl introduced herself as Maryanne James.

Dad nudged me, grinning. I took a step away from him. He'd already totally shamed me in front of my new roommate. There was no way I wanted Maryanne James getting the wrong idea about me.

Maryanne pointed to the rectangular-shaped sandstone building with the huge wooden doors, explaining that the school administration offices, nurses' station (my turn to nudge Dad), assembly hall, principal's office and staffrooms were all located at the front. 'Most of the classrooms are along each wing. Juniors on the right, seniors on the left. Year Twelve girls get their own common room,' she added with a satisfied grin.

I raised my hand, unable to contain myself a minute longer. 'Will we get to see the stables?'

'Rider?' Maryanne asked.

I nodded. 'You bet!'

'That's what I like to hear,' she said, then turned back to the rest of the group. 'Specialist rooms are at the back of the building. Drama, dance, art, science labs, kitchens—'

'How about the stables?' I piped up.

Maryanne smiled. 'How long has it been since they picked up your horse?'

'Twenty-four hours,' Dad announced. 'And hasn't she been driving us mad. It's been nothing but *Honey this* and *Honey that* and *Is she safe* and *Have they fed her?* The sooner she gets to the stables the better off we'll all be.'

Everyone laughed — except me. I'd never wanted to inflict actual pain on my father before, but there was a first time for everything. My face burned and I shot Dad the most poisonous look in my repertoire, the kind I usually saved for Carly, Queen of the Creeps.

'What?' He shrugged, looking as innocent as a newborn foal.

'Follow me,' Maryanne said.

The girl who'd smiled at me earlier, the one with the glasses, winked then set off after Maryanne, accompanied by her parents and a bored-looking older brother clutching a black electronic game.

I stomped after the crowd, the sound of their laughter still ringing in my ears.

Maryanne showed us the tennis courts, gymnasium and playing fields. There was a huge library, a drama theatre and an art gallery. There was a three-storey music centre that included a concert hall. (Mum had told me that I was starting violin lessons whether I liked it or not, despite my protests about horsehair bows.) Further along were netball and basketball courts and a rowing shed. (Linley rowers got up at 5 am, four mornings a week, to train on the river!) The whole crowd 'oohed', 'ahhed' and 'wowed' at the indoor pool. But not me. I was in torment — an entire day without my Honey horse and not a stable to be seen.

Maryanne must have read my mind. 'Next stop, Linley's unique equestrian centre,' she said.

'Yes!' I shouted, punching the air.

Everyone stared at me. The girl with the glasses giggled. Dad rolled his eyes.

I grinned sheepishly. 'Sorry. Horses are my thing.'

Maryanne raised her eyebrows. 'So I see.'

She walked on, the crowd following her like hungry ponies after a bucket of oats. Finally, there it was. I stared, amazed.

Sure, I'd read the brochure and asked questions at my interview and written a letter to the registrar and pored over the school website. But to see it all laid out here in front of me was incredible. I could see the indoor arena and caught the glint of sunlight on the mirrored corner. There was an outdoor sand arena, a rubber practice arena and a full-sized dressage arena. I counted ten day yards with stables and could see a long covered row of stalls. There was a huge barn for feed storage, and I could tell by the bars on the windows of a smaller building that it had to be the tack room. I knew that somewhere behind the complex were a cross-country course and a polocrosse field. I also knew there were paddocks for the agisted horses, for the school horses and several smaller quarantine yards for new horses. Honey was sure to be in one of those. I couldn't wait to see her.

'Linley's equestrian program is one of a kind — it's the only school in the country that lets students keep and ride their horses on site,' Maryanne explained. 'And, of course, Linley offers Equine Studies as part of the curriculum.'

I could see Glasses-girl whispering frantically to her parents. They shook their heads. Her brother yawned loudly and fidgeted with his game.

'Girls can start their riding lessons from kindergarten and continue right up until Year Twelve. Like me.' Maryanne smiled. 'Years Seven to Ten can elect to do Horsemanship, and then Equine Studies in Years Eleven and Twelve.'

Maryanne led us into the complex. I could instantly tell the horsy from the non-horsy. Several girls — myself and Glasses-girl among them — rushed to climb the white post-and-rail fence, hanging over as far as we could go without falling. The rest either stood with their arms folded looking bored, or clung to their parents in fear.

'Get down, Emily. This second!' called Glasses-girl's mother.

Emily hopped down from the fence and her mother brushed at her clothes with her hands. I could make out the words 'dirty' and 'behave'. Emily's face flushed red and she stood behind her parents. Her brother poked her with his game.

'Linley's facilities are second to none,' Maryanne said. 'Shows are held here at least once a month and Linley hosts the polocrosse state titles every year.'

I could see a few horses dotted across a series of small yards beyond the main area and strained for a glimpse of Honey.

'Linley has produced some of the best riders in the country,' Maryanne went on. 'And not only riders, by the way. Girls can graduate from Linley Heights with qualifications in stable management and practical horse care. Our riding staff are highly experienced. Some are actually Old Girls who completed their equestrian studies and returned to Linley to teach.' Maryanne swelled with pride. 'Like my sister, Demi.'

I made out four chestnut legs under a familiar-looking white cotton combo (a rug that covers a horse's neck as well as its body). The legs and combo were attached to a head that was nibbling at a patch of green.

It was her! It had to be her.

'Honey!' I shrieked, forgetting everything I'd ever been taught about calmness and quietness around horses. 'Honey, I'm over here!'

The chestnut raised her head and whinnied.

'Honey!' I waved both arms at her, barely noticing the laughter. I turned to Maryanne. 'How do I get to her?'

Maryanne pulled a mobile phone from her pocket and glanced at the screen. 'It's almost time for the welcoming address.'

I felt desperate. If Maryanne didn't understand me and my 'horse thing', who else would? 'Please! Just for a minute.' I gave her my look — the one that always works on Dad, no matter what. I just needed a quick Honey fix and I'd feel better. Maybe even good enough to sleep in the same room as Claire Carlson.

Maryanne gave me a smile and I knew I was in.

'Five minutes,' she said. 'Just run down to that gate. Make sure you close up after yourself, though.'

I jumped up and down, clapping my hands. 'Thanks! Thanks so much!'

I didn't wait for her to change her mind. I didn't even wait for Dad's okay. I ran to the gate, my fingers fumbling with the steel chain. I threw open the gate, closed it behind me again and reattached the chain. Then I ran past the first yard, then the second and the third. Finally I reached her. I leaped onto the fence and leaned in.

'Honey!' I said. 'Honey, it's me!'

She looked up at me and nickered. Then she raised her head and whinnied, trotting to the fence. I swung one leg over, then the other, and jumped to the ground, wrapping my arms around my Honey horse's neck.

'Oh, Honey, it's so good to see you!' I squeezed her, rubbing my cheek against her, feeling her warmth and breathing in her smell. 'How've they been treating you?'

I checked her water trough and found that it was full. Her feed bin was empty, but traces of rich green lucerne hay lying around it told me she'd had her breakfast. I looked at my watch, wondering when they were given their afternoon feed, then scratched at Honey's forelock, promising her I'd be there to feed her myself. I had to make sure she got the slices of carrot in her dinner that she liked so much. Then I checked that her rug was properly buckled and her fly mask was sitting comfortably around her ears. I ran my hands down each of her legs, feeling for swelling or heat, then gently squeezed the tendon on the back of each leg, asking her to lift her feet. I cursed myself for not bringing my hoof pick as I hacked away at the mud with my fingers.

'What're you doin' in there?'

I was jolted out of my delicious horsy moment by a gruff voice. I set Honey's foot down and spun around. A man, not much taller than me, was watching me with a pair of very dark eyes. He looked to be older than Dad and was wearing heavy work boots and a broad-brimmed hat. His skin was covered with freckles.

I opened and closed my mouth a few times, but no sound came out.

'I … uh … I …' I backed into Honey. If this guy was after my horse, he'd have to get past me first.

'This horse is in quarantine. You shouldn't be in there.' The man tipped his hat and scratched at his forehead.

'How long does she have to be in here for?'

The man smiled. 'All new horses are isolated

from the other horses for the first few days. We worm 'em, check 'em for mites and the like, for strangles, check their poo—'

'Their *poo*?' I was shocked. 'Why?'

The man laughed. 'Don't you check poo?'

I shook my head.

'You know how you can go to a doctor and get yourself put on one of those fancy machines and it gives you a reading of your heart and blood and all that?'

This time I nodded.

'A horse's poo is like that. We can find out a heap about a horse's health from its poo. We can even work out what kind of grass it's been eating.'

My eyes were wide. 'You're kidding.'

'I'm serious.' The man leaned on Honey's fence. Now he was closer I could see the Linley Heights crest embroidered on his polo shirt. Underneath it was his name in yellow stitching, JOE, and the word STAFF. 'If you take a look at this mare's poo, you'll see it's a nice golden colour. Nice shape too. Means she's been gettin' plenty of good green grass. Grass is mostly water of course, and when a horse eats dry grass — a lot of that around now, with this drought — her poo can be a real dark green. A

39

horse on too-dry grass could become prone to colic and we wouldn't—'

'Ashleigh!'

I heard my name and waved at Dad. He shook his head and made a 'T' with his hands.

'I've gotta go,' I told Joe. 'What time's the afternoon feed?'

'We start at three thirty. Finish up about five.'

I smiled. 'I'll be back!'

Joe frowned. 'You still haven't told me what you were doing with this mare's feet.'

I stuck out my hand. 'I'm Ashleigh Miller and this is my horse, Honey.'

Joe nodded, smiling, and shook my hand. 'Riding student, eh?'

I nodded.

'Expect I'll be seein' a lot of you round these parts, then.'

'Ash! Get a move on, will you?'

I looked over at the tour group. Maryanne James was leading them back towards the main building. Dad was standing on the fence now, waving both his arms above his head.

I said goodbye, first to Honey and then to Joe, and ran back to Dad. He wasted no time in grabbing my hand and yanking me back to the tour group, muttering to himself about brain shrinkage. We had an appointment with Mrs Freeman, the principal, in a minute and a half. My life at Linley Heights was just about to begin.

five

Welcome to Linley

'Is this seat taken? Can I sit here?'

I twisted around mid-text to Becky, telling her how cool the riding centre was, to find Emily from the school tour smiling down at me. I shook my head as I pressed 'send', then said, 'No.'

Emily's smile vanished. 'Was that *No, this seat's not taken* or *No, you can't sit here*?'

I slapped my forehead. 'I meant it's not taken, so please sit here.'

I was alone. Dad had decided I needed to find my feet at Linley while he found the bathroom. Needless to say he'd got lost and I was all nervy inside. If Emily wanted to sit beside me, that was great.

Emily grinned and slipped into the seat. She held out her hand. 'Emily Phuong.'

I grabbed her hand and shook it. 'Ashleigh Miller.'

'This is some assembly hall, eh?'

Emily was right. It was built like a theatre with a stage, an orchestra pit and raised seating (we were sitting about halfway up). The walls were decorated with paintings by artists whose work you'd expect to see in an art gallery in the city, not in a school. There were six long stained-glass windows on either side of the hall depicting Australian scenes that made me swell with pride, like Sydney's Opera House and Harbour Bridge, Canberra's Parliament House, our wildlife and the outback. There were portraits of women like Dame Enid Lyons, the first woman elected to the Australian Federal Parliament, and Evonne Goolagong Cawley, a Wimbledon champion. I also recognized Vicki Roycroft — of course! There was a banner running along the wall behind the stage with five words printed on it: *Integrity, Excellence, Innovation, Courage, Community*. On the stage was a dark wooden podium with the Linley Heights crest on the front and a microphone on top. I stared and stared, feeling like the smallest creature on the planet.

Emily looked over each shoulder, slumped deep into her seat and sighed. 'Thank goodness!'

I frowned, confused. 'Thank goodness what?'

'I've lost my brother. He's kind of a pain. He doesn't talk any more, only grunts. Mum reckons it's hormones and he should be over it by the time he's seventy-three.' Emily rolled her eyes. 'Have you got a brother?'

'Yeah, but he's just a baby. This is him.' I pressed a few buttons on my brand-new mobile phone and showed Emily my latest photo of Jason. He was all smiles, two baby teeth and fat red cheeks.

'He's so sweet!' she said. 'But I'm warning you. They all turn into boys in the end.'

'I wanted a sister, but I'm used to him now.' I pocketed my phone.

Emily laughed. 'I've got one of those too. Mercedes. She's in Year Ten this year, right here at Linley. I call her Murk, but she doesn't know that!'

'How cool!' I said. 'Your own sister at the same school. I'll never get to be at school with Jase.'

'Are you serious?' Emily said. 'She made me sign a contract before we left home. I'm never allowed to talk to her in public. If we happen to walk past each other I'm s'posed to pretend I don't know her. She can talk to me whenever she wants, of course.'

I raised my eyebrows. 'What happens if you break the contract?'

Emily sighed again. 'She said she'd shave off my eyebrows while I was asleep.'

My eyes went wide. 'Wow.'

'Wow's right. I kind of like my eyebrows where they are.'

I nudged Emily. Mrs Freeman, principal of Linley Heights School, was an elegant woman with short golden hair. She was wearing a beautiful cream suit and was standing at the podium. Silence fell over the entire hall like a New Zealand rug over a pony. Mrs Freeman introduced herself to the assembled parents and girls in a quiet, controlled voice.

'Welcome,' she said, 'to those returning to our school, and a special welcome to those joining us for the first time.'

Emily and I beamed at one another.

After Mrs Freeman's speech, we all stood and sang the national anthem and the Linley Heights school song (lucky for Em and me the words were up above the stage on a screen), and the welcoming assembly was over.

My brain felt stuffed. 'I don't think I can fit any more in here,' I said, rubbing my head. 'When do we get our first weekend off campus? I think I need one already.'

'Wait 'til the homework starts,' Emily said. 'Murk even gets it in the holidays.'

'Are they allowed to do that?' I was shocked. In my entire life I'd never once had holiday homework.

'Welcome to Linley Heights!' Emily grinned, her glasses shining.

We joined the crowd of parents and girls shuffling out of the assembly hall. Lunch was being served in the boarders' dining room and nobody wanted to miss out. I could smell the food from here and my mouth was already watering.

On the way to lunch Emily told me a bit about herself. She was the youngest in her family, and they lived in a town about three hours away called Barton where her mum and dad ran the local pharmacy. (Mercedes loved the discount on nail polish.) Like her sister, Emily was at Linley to become a doctor or a lawyer.

'They'd even be happy with both,' she groaned.

'What do you want to do?' I said as we found a

table and sat down opposite each other. There was a family already there, surrounding a weeping girl. 'When you grow up, I mean?'

Emily shrugged. 'Not sure. I mean, I want to make them happy. But all I ever wanted was to be a vet. What about you?'

I picked up a bread roll and pressed it against my nose, inhaling deeply. 'As long as it's something to do with horses, I don't care.'

Emily smiled. 'I noticed you have a bit of a horse thing going on.'

I nodded. 'I have a lot of a horse thing. Hey!' I wriggled in my seat, overwhelmed by the incredible brilliance of my latest incredibly brilliant idea. 'Why don't you come and meet Honey after lunch? I know she'd love you.'

Emily shrugged. 'I'd love to, but …'

'But what?'

She leaned across the table. 'I'm not s'posed to go near the horses.'

I frowned. 'Why not?'

Em shrugged again, her cheeks darkening. 'Mum hates horses. She reckons I could get hurt.'

I was flabbergasted. 'What about you? Do you hate them?'

Emily shook her head, her eyes bright. 'I love 'em. That's why I was so totally happy to come to Linley — even though it's boarding and even though I have to put up with Murk. My brother's lucky to get away from her. He's boarding at King George.'

'I hope King George doesn't mind!'

Emily giggled. 'It's this school for boys. It's really old and looks like a castle. Some kids reckon it's haunted by the ghosts of the convicts that had to build it.'

'Cool!' I said. 'You think we have any ghosts here?'

Emily shivered. 'Hope not.'

A trolley arrived, pushed by a Linley girl wearing a dark blue apron (Linley-crested, of course) over her uniform and a sour face. (I found out later that all houses took turns on the serving roster.) She passed plates of lasagne and salad down the table. The weeping girl pushed her plate away immediately.

'D'you ride?' I picked up a fork, my mouth practically dripping.

Emily shook her head. 'No. But I really wanna learn.'

I smiled, a plan forming in my head. 'You've got six years.'

'No way!' Emily said. 'Mum'd kill me. If the horse didn't kill me first! Sounds like something she'd say, actually!'

'How's she ever gonna find out?' I said, slicing off a huge chunk of lasagne.

'Murk,' Emily hissed. 'The Global News Service herself. I can't do anything without her telling Mum and Dad.'

I offered Emily my pinky. 'We'll just have to make sure she doesn't catch us then, won't we?'

Emily dropped her knife and fork, ignoring her lunch. 'What are you saying?'

'You wanna learn and I can teach you. It'll be fun!'

Emily rubbed her hands against her arms as if she was cold. 'I don't know.'

'Aw, come on,' I said. 'It'll be fun, and I promise nothing'll go wrong. Just trust me, okay?'

Emily hooked her pinky around mine. 'Okay.'

We shook on it.

'Ash! Where have you been? I've been looking everywhere for you! I was worried out of my head — is that lasagne?'

I giggled. 'Emily, this is my dad.'

'Nice to meet you, Mr … uh?'

'Miller,' I reminded her.

Dad and Emily shook hands and he gestured at my lunch. 'Where do you think I can get myself one of those?' He wandered away accompanied by the clink and scrape of knives and forks on fast-emptying plates.

'Do you know anyone else here?' I asked Emily.

She rolled her eyes. 'Only Murk's friends. They're as bad as her. So, apart from my horrible sister and her equally horrible friends, there's no one I know here but you.'

I grinned, my teeth smeared with sticky tomatoey goo. 'We'd better stick together then, eh?'

Emily grimaced. 'On one condition.'

'Anything.'

'Clean your teeth!'

Emily collapsed in giggles. I did the same.

'What are you two laughing about?' said a sweet voice.

Emily didn't even look up. 'Get lost, Mercedes.'

I tapped Em's hand. Whoever it was looking down at us, she didn't look like a candidate for Mercedes Phuong. She had green eyes, long, straight blonde hair that could've given a waterfall a run for its money in the cascade department, and wore a yellow and green jacket emblazoned with the words *Australian National Youth Equestrian Team*.

'Who are you?' Emily said, a piece of lettuce hanging limply from her fork.

The girl gave a smile as sweet as her voice. 'India McCray. I understand one of you is Ashleigh Miller.'

I raised my hand a little, not really sure if I wanted to own up to being the only Ashleigh Miller at the table. India rested her cool, green-as-a-paddock-after-a-good-summer-rain eyes on me. I had a feeling she was weighing me up. It wasn't pleasant.

'What can I do for you?' I said.

'You can tell me something,' India replied. 'Are you the riding scholarship recipient?'

I shrugged. 'Yeah.'

She smiled again. Like a cat this time. A cat that's eaten a canary. 'Interesting. They must have changed the criteria this year.'

I felt prickly. Not that I wanted to. I remembered how I'd promised myself to be friends with everyone at my new school. But it looked like India wasn't interested in helping me keep my promise.

'What's that supposed to mean?' I said.

She smiled again, sweet as molasses. 'Nothing! Nothing at all. Look, it was great to meet you, Andy.'

Emily's eyes widened and she sucked in her breath.

'It's Ashleigh,' I said, but India had already turned her back on me and was walking away.

'Can you believe her?' Em said. 'Must be a friend of Murk's.'

I sighed and pushed my plate away.

'Don't let her turn you off your lunch,' Emily said fiercely, so worked up her glasses were steamy. 'Believe me, there're plenty more where she comes from.'

I looked around the dining hall at the enormous arched windows and the long wooden tables where generations of Linley girls had come together to eat. My throat swelled and my eyes stung. I knew what was coming and dipped my head so my new friend wouldn't see me blub.

'Homesick?' Emily said gently. Then her face changed. 'Or was it that blondey kid who upset you? Where did she go? I'll fix her!'

I shook my head. I was homesick, but I was upset now as well. I'd thought that being the only riding scholarship winner in Year Seven would be a badge of honour, that the other girls would like me and want to be my friend. But I understood exactly the meaning behind India's words. She didn't think I was good enough for Linley. And she hadn't even seen me ride. It wasn't fair. A tear ran down my face and I wiped it away quickly with my serviette.

Emily drew her perfect black eyebrows together in a frown. 'As far as I can see, Ash, you have two options. You can sit here crying into your lasagne or you can stick it to that India kid. Don't let her walk all over you. Show her what you're made of!'

I smiled weakly. 'You're on.'

Emily beamed. 'That's more like it.'

Em and I stacked our plates on the same silver trolley that had brought us our lunch. It was time to say goodbye to our parents and hello to high school and the whole new Linley Heights world. Hello to homework and teachers and bells and roommates. Hello to new friends like Em, and some who didn't seem so friendly. Hello to uniforms and panama hats and assemblies and houses. And, best of all, hello to riding at school and Horsemanship classes and stable management lessons and polocrosse matches.

Nothing and nobody was going to ruin Linley for me, I decided. Not even India McCray and Claire Carlson. I thought about Becky and Jenna and Pree, about Mum, Dad and Jason. I thought about Holly, my first riding teacher, and Mrs Strickland from Waratah Grove and Mrs Mac from Shady Trails who'd done so much to get me to Linley in the first place. I thought about them all and made a vow: I was going to make them proud. With Honey by my side, and now Em too, I could do it. I *would* do it. I owed it to them. I owed it to myself.

six

Sticky Honey

'That was some night,' I said to Emily the next day at breakfast. Linley had put on a feast of bacon, eggs, sausages, fried tomato and toast and Em and I were as starved as the food was delicious.

'What happened?' Em said. 'Did you see a ghost?'

'Worse — Claire sleepwalks!' I was barely able to believe it myself. 'I heard this noise in the night and woke up, and there she was, vacuuming. In her sleep! Then when I woke up this morning, there was this hissing sound and she was spraying me!'

'What for?' Emily was stunned. The sausage she'd stabbed with her fork hung, half-eaten, near her mouth.

'You know how I took you to meet Honey last night? Well, Claire reckons I brought dirt into the room. I reckon she's one of those clean freaks.'

Em shook her head. 'There's gotta be a rule against that sort of thing.'

I pulled a face. 'According to her, there're plenty of rules — against people like me! She's not letting me forget that her mum's president of the Parents' Association.'

I filled Emily in on the Carlsons' plans to close down the riding program.

'That's evil!' Em said, dropping her sausage. 'They can't pull the plug on the riding program. It makes Linley special. Take the horses away and what's left? Linley Heights'll be just like every other boarding school in the country.'

'It's up to us to stop them then,' I said, determined.

Emily offered her pinky. I shook it.

'So what's your roommate like?' I scooped up some scrambled egg.

Emily beamed. 'Anna's nice. She's from Port Alfred, about four hours north of here. Snores like you wouldn't believe, though.'

'I'd rather a snorer than a sprayer any day.'

'At least Miss Stephens is nice.' Emily sliced her bacon down the middle.

Miss Stephens was our boarding house mistress. Well, one of them. There were so many boarders we needed a mistress for each form.

'She showed me how to ring home,' I said. 'Which made things worse.'

Emily frowned. 'How?'

'I was homesick enough as it was. Hearing their voices was the last straw.'

I'd been okay until bedtime. But then I started thinking about Mum and Dad and Jason and what they would be doing. Mum would have been giving Jason a bath and Dad would have been washing up. If I'd been there, he'd have flicked my behind with the tea towel and chased me upstairs to bed. Then I'd thought about Toffee and how lonely he must be without Honey and me. And about Becky and how in only one day's time she'd be starting at Shady Creek and Districts High School without me. So I'd SMSed Becky to wish her luck, then called home to say goodnight and check on Toff and make sure Mum had given him his dinner. Mum had cried and put Jase on the phone, and he'd made his gurgly baby noise, which made me cry even more than

Mum. Getting to sleep in a strange bed in a strange room with a strange roommate had been pretty hard after that.

Em patted my hand and smiled. 'Things'll get easier. We'll get used to it here. Everyone says it takes a while, but then it just seems normal and you feel all out of place when you go back home.'

'That'll never happen to me,' I said. 'I love Shady Creek.'

We both swallowed the last of our breakfast and wondered what to do with the day. It was a Monday, our last day of freedom before the day girls arrived and lessons began.

Em looked at her watch. 'We've got the whole day free. Trust me when I tell you this'll never happen again. They're lulling us into a false sense of relaxation.'

'I don't know about you, but I just got a craving for Honey!'

'Yes!' Emily punched the air.

Half an hour later we were jogging down to the riding centre. Joe had finally convinced me that my tack would be safe in the alarmed, barred-windowed, strictly-off-limits-to-non-riding-students tack room. Well, sort of convinced me. But not having to lug my grooming kit, helmet, crop, lunge line, lunging whip, cavesson, saddle, bridle and saddlecloth the fifteen-minute walk from the boarding house to the riding centre every day, sometimes twice a day, was certainly appealing. Even to me. And Claire was euphoric about not having my horsy gear in our room.

'We'll make sure Honey's had her breakfast, then give her a good groom. Ever groomed a horse before?' I asked Em. I'd collected my grooming kit from the tack room and was ready to brush.

Em shook her head. 'Never. Mum'd have a ginormous fit if she knew I was even thinking about going near the horses, much less touching one. Speaking of which.' Emily looked over each shoulder. 'Seen Murk anywhere? Remember what I said to you. Her eyes, ears and mouth are directly connected to Mum's.'

I stopped mid-jog and climbed up on the nearest fence. There was no sign of anyone anywhere.

'Can't see anyone,' I said. 'But even if I could, I don't know what your sister looks like.'

'A whole lot like me,' Em said seriously. 'But she's got ears like funnels and a mouth like a megaphone. Oh, and twenty-twenty vision.'

'It can't be that bad,' I said, swallowing my giggles.

Emily rolled her eyes. 'It can be. And it is.'

I jumped down from the fence and held out my hand. 'Will you trust me?'

Em nodded and grabbed my hand, squeezing hard. 'Sure.'

I tugged on her arm. 'Then let's go. Your first riding lesson awaits!'

We jogged past the paddocks to the row of small private yards I'd visited the day before. I waved to Joe, who was bent double over a grey pony's hoof with a mouth full of nails. He nodded a 'hello'.

When we reached Honey, she nickered and hung her head over the gate, pushing her nose into my hand for a titbit.

'Nothing today,' I said. 'Sorry!'

I was lying. My pockets were crammed full of slices of carrot and Honey could smell them. She stamped her foot and tossed her head, her nostrils flaring.

'Okay, okay!' I held up my hands. 'You win. Em, wanna give her a carrot?'

Emily beamed. 'Cool! But how?'

'Here.' I passed her a slice of carrot and

demonstrated the best way to hold her hand: flat, with fingers pointing down, and the carrot in the centre of her palm.

'There's a trick to it,' I said. 'You kinda push the carrot in. Stops you getting your fingers bitten off.'

Emily went pale. 'Bitten off? Mum'll find out I went near the horses for sure if I go home with four less fingers.'

I laughed. 'I'm only kidding, Em. Most horses only eat one finger at a time.'

Emily gave me a look. 'Funny.'

'Give it a go, then.'

She held out her hand and Honey took the carrot. Em giggled in delight as Honey crunched. 'Wow! My first time.'

'It's gonna be a day of firsts for you.'

I opened the gate of Honey's yard and let myself in, gesturing to Emily to follow me. She was shaking with excitement.

'This is so cool,' she said. 'SO cool!'

'Catch her,' I told her, holding out Honey's halter and lead rope.

Emily pointed to herself, her eyes wide. 'Me? Catch a horse?'

'You bet.'

She took the halter and examined it. 'But how do I get it on her? It looks like some kind of rope puzzle.'

'Easy. See that circle piece?' I pointed to the noseband of the halter. Em nodded. 'You slip that over her nose and bring the strap behind her ears then buckle it up, like a shoe, at her cheek.'

'Sounds like fun.'

I smiled. 'That's coz it is fun. Now give it a try.'

'Okay.' Em shrugged, half-nervous.

'Don't be afraid,' I coached. 'Horses can tell instantly if you're scared and they get scared too. Horses look for a leader, and if you're afraid or timid they'll make themselves leader.'

'I'm not afraid!' Emily said. 'I'm not afraid of anything.'

'Except Murky finding out you're here. Hey, put this on.' I passed Em my red Shady Trails cap and jacket. 'Your sister'll never recognize you now. Feel better?'

Em nodded. 'Much.'

'Now, catch your mare.'

I leaned on the fence, watching. Ready to jump at the first sign of danger to Em or Honey.

Emily approached Honey's right side, or offside.

'Wrong side,' I said. 'We do everything on the horse's left, her nearside.'

'Nearside, right.'

'No, left. Your right.'

'I'm right on the left?'

'Her left,' I said. 'Right!'

Em threw up her hands.

'I see you know where to look for the horse gods already!' I said and laughed.

Emily scowled. 'The first thing I'll ask them for is to make me less confused.'

'This horse isn't gonna catch herself,' I said.

Emily gave me a look. I grinned at her, my hands on my hips.

She stepped towards Honey's near shoulder and patted her neck, then stooped down and gently pulled the noseband of the halter over her nose, resting it in exactly the right place on her face.

'That's the way!' I said. 'Now buckle it up and you've got her.'

Em fed the earpiece strap into the buckle. Honey tossed her head and the halter slipped to the ground. She stamped on it and trotted away across the yard.

'Watcha doing, girl?' I said, scooping the halter from the ground. 'Sorry, Em. She's never done anything like that before.'

Emily shrugged. 'Maybe it's me. Maybe she doesn't like me or something.'

'Of course she likes you.'

I took a few steps toward Honey's nearside. She saw me coming and dashed to the opposite side of the yard. I made a grab for her rug and missed entirely. 'Honey!'

Emily giggled. 'Maybe she doesn't like you.'

'She loves me,' I said. 'She's s'posed to, anyway.'

I approached her again, making soothing sounds. She bounced away. I tried again, this time making sounds that weren't so much soothing as annoyed.

'Honey, cut it out!' I said, chasing her from corner to corner. My horse, still not tired of the game, held her head and tail high, snorting in delight. 'What's wrong with you?'

Honey had nothing to say, she just leaped across the yard again, whinnying.

'Havin' trouble, Miss?'

I spun around. Joe was leaning on the gate watching me, a look of amusement on his face.

I groaned, exasperated. 'I dunno what's got into this horse! I've never had a problem catching her. Ever!'

Joe shrugged. 'Tried looking at it from the filly's point of view, Miss …?'

'Ashleigh,' I said, grouchy. 'What do you mean, her point of view?'

'How long's she been with you?'

'Over a year,' I said. 'Nearly a year and a half.'

'And before that?'

I told Joe the whole story. About how I'd found Honey half-starved and nearly dead on a dusty property and rescued her, making her well again and making her mine.

'Well then,' Joe said. 'So she's been through a whole lotta trauma, then settled in nicely with you at home, and now she finds herself in a new place with new smells and horses and faces. No, Ashleigh. It's not the filly's fault.'

'I guess.' My shoulders slumped. I'd been trying to teach my new friend about horses and I hadn't thought about how my own horse might be feeling. 'But she's been away from home before. For four weeks. At Waratah Grove.'

'Waratah Grove, eh? How's old Mrs Strickland?'

'She's good. But what's wrong with Honey? Why would she be okay there and not here?'

'D'you always feel the same way? Think and react the same way?'

I shook my head.

'Well, neither do horses.' Joe opened the gate. 'Want me to have a crack at it?'

I shrugged. 'Whatever you think.'

Joe approached Honey quietly, moving towards her diagonally and holding out his hand.

'Why are you walking like that?' Emily asked.

'Well, I've been workin' with these animals a lot of years and my experience tells me that if you wanna have any kinda luck with 'em, you gotta try understandin' 'em. Humans are meat eaters, which means they smell like meat and they move like predators — in a straight line.'

'What's that got to do with catching a horse?' I said.

'Everything.' Joe waved away a fly with his hand — the 'Aussie salute' as Mum calls it. 'Horses are prey animals. When they feel they're being hunted, their instincts tell 'em to run away.

'But if you approach 'em as another horse would, rather than as a meat-eating hunter would, you might just increase your chances of catching one!'

I couldn't believe no one had ever told me that before. And it worked. Joe looped the lead rope around Honey's neck, then slipped the noseband of the halter over her face and buckled it at her cheek. He held the lead rope under her chin and led her to me. 'Special delivery.'

I took the lead rope. 'Thanks.'

'No worries at all,' Joe said, letting himself out of the gate. 'Your filly prob'ly needs a little time to adjust, that's all.'

I led Honey to the fence and secured her lead rope to one of the loops of brightly coloured twine flapping in the morning breeze.

'Ready for your first grooming lesson?' I asked Emily, who was picking her way through my grooming kit.

'Hope it goes better than my first catching lesson. Wowsers — this horse has more brushes than Murk!'

'Needs every one of 'em too,' I said. 'She has her own make-up as well, for shows.'

Emily stared, wide-eyed. 'Horses wear make-up?'

'Sure,' I said, selecting a red-handled hoof pick with a built-in brush from my kit. 'I rub white chalk into all her white markings to make them stand out, and dark oil on her chestnuts and legs so they shine, and there's this special shampoo I use on the day before a show that makes her coat really gleam, and of course there's mane and tail detangler and after-grooming spray to make them really sparkle, and—'

'What's a chestnut?' Emily said. 'Isn't that a colour?'

I nodded, running my hand down the back of Honey's near foreleg and squeezing her tendon gently. She lifted her foot without a problem, making me even more confused about her earlier behaviour. 'Sure it's a colour — Honey's colour! But chestnuts are also those funny, shell-shaped knobbly bits of skin inside a horse's legs. Now c'mon, Em.'

Emily joined me and I showed her how to clean Honey's feet, gently scraping out mud, rocks and manure away from her toe, avoiding her sensitive triangular-shaped frog.

'She's almost due for shoeing,' I said, peering closely at the foot I was holding.

'How often does she need new shoes?' Emily asked, running her finger along Honey's shoe.

'About every six weeks. The hoof keeps growing, like our fingernails. They're made of the same sort of stuff too. Anyway, they need to be trimmed back so they're neat and comfortable for the horse. The shoes wear down as well.'

'Do they really need shoes? Wild horses don't wear 'em.'

'Heaps of horses go barefoot,' I said, shrugging. 'But being shod or unshod depends on so many things. Like the work the horse is gonna do, if the ground is hard or soft, what they're eating, how hard their hoof is naturally … Owners just have to weigh it up. Usually horses with white feet have to wear shoes, whether their owners want them to or not. White hooves aren't as hard as black ones.'

Emily collapsed onto the edge of Honey's water trough. 'Double wowsers. There's so much to think about with horses!'

'Tell me about it,' I said, laughing. 'My whole life revolves around Honey. But she's worth it. Some people were just born to love horses and I'm one of them.'

'Well, some people were born to love chocolate and I'm one of them.' Emily pulled a half-melted, oddly shaped chocolate bar in shiny wrapping from her back pocket. 'Want some?'

I shook my head. 'Not now I know where it's been all morning. Brushes!'

I laid one of each type of Honey's brushes on the ground, explaining as I went. 'That black one's a rubber currycomb for removing mud. Don't be too rough with it on a bony part of the horse, specially their legs. That one, with the long bristles, is a dandy-brush for the whole body and mane and tail. It gets out a lot of dirt. This one with the shorter, softer bristles is a body brush, for finishing the job and adding shine.'

'What about this one, with the sponge inside?'

'You use that for shampooing.' I poked the spongy part of the brush. 'You squeeze the shampoo here and rub it all over the horse. Much easier than rubbing it in with your hands, trust me.'

Under my instruction (and once the chocolate had been carefully licked from each finger), Emily completed her very first groom of a horse.

She collapsed on the water trough again, exhausted, but proud. 'Dunno how this is gonna help me become a lawyer but it was heaps of fun.'

I frowned, pushing the lid down hard on my kit. 'Do you really wanna be a lawyer, Em?'

She shook her head. 'Nuh.'

'What do you wanna do, then?'

She shrugged. 'Don't know. But I love animals. I always kinda wanted to be a vet.'

'A vet's a doctor. Wouldn't they be happy with that?'

She shrugged again. 'We'll see. Look who's here.'

It was India McCray, wearing her yellow and green jacket and walking her chestnut gelding past Honey's yard. I chewed on my bottom lip. There was something about India having a chestnut too that made me nervous. India pulled her horse up and gave me a smile. The kind you give when you're not really smiling.

'Elly,' she said.

'It's Ashleigh.'

'This your horse?'

'This yours?'

Her smile vanished. 'Heard you couldn't even get a halter on it earlier. I'd keep a close eye on that scholarship of yours. Someone might just take it from you.'

I was shocked. 'What do you mean?'

'If you'd been here since kindergarten like me, you'd know that if the scholarship recipient is a failure she can be stripped of her entitlements. The privileges and full remission of fees will be passed on to the next most suitable applicant.'

I swallowed hard. It sounded like India had memorized the Linley rule book. I'd believed from the start that the scholarship was mine, would always be mine, but now my heart pumped harder and faster. What if I failed at Linley? Would I have to leave? Did I have to come top of my academic classes too, or just be good at riding? I imagined Honey and me having to limp back to Shady Creek, our tails between our legs, admitting to everyone that we were losers. I felt all swoony just thinking about it. Carly and her fellow Creepketeers would make my life a misery. How would I face Mrs Mac? And what about my parents? They were so proud. I was the only person in my whole family ever to go to boarding school. How could I tell them I'd been kicked out?

'So what's your problem?' Emily asked India, her hands on her hips. 'The fact that Ash got the scholarship and you didn't, or the fact that she's starting in Year Seven and you've been here the whole time? Or is it both?'

India's cold green eyes rested on Emily's face. 'I'd watch it if I were you. I might just happen to let it slip to your sister that I saw you at the riding centre.'

It was Emily's turn to be shocked. 'But how—'

'Not much happens around here that I don't know about. Not much happens around here that I don't make happen. So be careful, both of you.' She gave us one last fake smile and urged her horse on.

I shuddered. 'Breed 'em tough around here, don't they?'

Em's face was pale. 'Ash, I gotta get out of here!'

'But your lesson — you were gonna have your first ride.'

She shook her head. 'You ride. I'll meet you later.'

With that, she slipped between the fence posts and ran back towards the school buildings.

I was scared and furious all at once. India McCray was everything I had hoped not to find at Linley. And I wasn't here for Sunday Riding Club or a four-week camp. It was a whole six years. Six years of India McCray. As long as I didn't lose my scholarship, that was. I grimaced, determined I'd never let it go. Not to anyone, but especially not to India. She could do or say or threaten anything. But she was never going to take it away from me. Not now. Not ever.

seven

Trouble from Day One

'So, how do I look?' I said to Claire, smoothing down the pleats at the front of my brand-new pale blue Linley Heights summer uniform. I admired myself in the mirror. For someone who'd been up since five and at the riding centre feeding, grooming and mucking out for an hour, I hadn't scrubbed up too badly. I rubbed at a splash of mud on my face and bared my teeth.

'Like you're crawling with germs,' Claire said from behind the jumper she was holding over her mouth and nose. 'You smell like a horse, as well.'

'Thanks!' I said. 'Wanna come and eat breakfast with me or would you rather stay here and disinfect my sheets?'

Claire gave me a look. There was a rap at the door and I swung it wide open.

'Looking good,' Em said, nodding at my uniform. 'You're a real Linley girl, now.'

'For how long, though?' I muttered.

'For as long as it takes my mum to close down the riding centre,' Claire said.

'If you don't like the horses, why don't you just leave?' Emily asked. 'Go to another school. A horseless one.'

Claire looked shocked. 'But I've been here since kindergarten.'

Emily rolled her eyes as we left the room, closing the door behind us. 'Another one. Is it just me or do all the been-here-since-kindy girls have an attitude problem?'

In the dining hall, India spotted us and lifted her chin. I noticed that Claire sat on the same side of the room as India. Was there a 'since kindy' side and a 'new girl' side? Would the two sides ever get along?

'Nervous about today?' Em asked, stuffing a fried egg into her mouth.

'That's disgusting,' I groaned, picking at my cereal. 'How can you eat that sort of thing today? I feel sick!'

She swallowed. 'I guess you are nervous then.'

We finished our breakfast and stacked our dishes on the trolley, then rushed back to our rooms to collect our schoolbags. The bell was about to ring and we were about to be late!

The assembly hall was full of Year Seven girls of all shapes, sizes and hair colours, boarders and day girls. I sat close to Emily, shaking in my brand-new school ... I looked down. Work boots! I'd gone to the riding centre that morning, come back, thrown on my uniform and forgotten to change my shoes!

I looked around, feeling panic rise in me like boiling water. No one else was wearing muddy work boots with bits of lucerne hay and probably horse manure embedded in the soles. Everyone else had on the regulation black lace-up shoes described in the Linley Heights handbook. I had to change.

I nudged Em and pointed at my feet. She covered her mouth with her hand, her eyes wide.

'They'll put you on uniform detention,' she hissed. 'Try to cover 'em up.'

'How?!'

I was horrified. How was I going to hang on to my scholarship if I got a detention on my first day? And what would happen to me in detention? Would I be locked in stocks and have wet sponges thrown at my head? Or would they skip that part and put me on the first train back to Shady Creek? There were a squillion possibilities. I didn't like any of them.

'Shh.' Emily pressed her index finger to her lips. 'Mrs Freeman.'

Everyone stood as the principal of Linley Heights stepped onto the stage. She was followed by a parade of teachers wearing long black gowns and funny flat hats. Following the teachers were the senior girls, all wearing hats, badges on their collars and blazers with words embroidered down the front, just like Maryanne James. I was amazed. They looked so much older than us. Would I ever be like them?

On Mrs Freeman's command we sang the school song:

Linley Heights girls grow in light
Ever striving, ever learning …

I could hear a few girls singing their own version and twisted around to see who they were.

Someone tapped my shoulder. I turned back around and came face to face with a flat hat.

'Eyes to the front,' it hissed.

I swallowed and nodded.

'Sing up!' the hat said.

'But I don't know—' I began.

'Don't answer back!' The hat was angry. 'Go and stand at the side of the hall.'

My face burned and my heart thumped as I squeezed past Emily and a few other girls. I stood where I was told to stand, feeling desperate. What if she (it was a lady hat) saw my shoes? What would happen to me then?

The school song finished and everyone sat down. Everyone but me. I could feel every eye on me. Every girl in Year Seven, every teacher on the stage, every big girl in a blazer. I wanted to disappear. I wanted Honey. I wanted my mum.

The hat drifted past me. 'Stay silent.'

I nodded, looking up at her. She looked back at me, her face red, deep lines around her mouth and eyes. Dad called them 'laugh lines', but I didn't think this teacher had laughed once in her whole life.

The assembly began. We were divided into one of eight houses, each named after a former school principal. I was put in Wilson, the same as India. Emily was in Bond. We would have roll call in our house groups every morning, go to chapel once a week, and get together for peer support where we got to talk to and do fun things with the older girls. We could earn points for our house by competing in sports and debating, for good school work and for good effort and behaviour. I was totally stoked to learn that we could earn mega points by competing in school and outside gymkhanas and shows. But I was unstoked when Mrs Freeman explained that points could be deducted for bad behaviour. India McCray caught my eye and clapped noiselessly. I wondered when the system started and hoped it was after the assembly! At the end of the year, the Linley Heights Cup would be awarded to the house that had earned the most points.

We were given our timetables. I stared at mine. It'd take me the whole year just to learn how to read it. We had six lessons a day plus an activity lesson (for peer support or assembly or chapel) before lunch. Each subject was taught in a different room and had its own teacher. There were the usual subjects like English and Maths (groan), and some I was dying to start — like Horsemanship, which consisted of two theory and two practical riding lessons per week! Then there were others I'd never done before, like Latin and Speech.

There was so much to think about. So much to remember. Somewhere outside a bell rang and we were dismissed for morning tea.

'I'm not hungry,' I said to Em as we shuffled outside. 'I'm gonna go change my shoes.'

Emily waved me goodbye and I ran off in the direction of the boarding house. Then I stopped. If I had time to change my shoes, surely I had time to visit my Honey horse as well. One quick visit couldn't hurt. Just a few minutes.

I jogged all the way to Honey's yard. It was empty.

My heart started to pound. Where was she? Had she run away? Had she been stolen? Had someone hidden her? Was she out there alone somewhere, lost and frightened?

'Lookin' for your filly?' said a familiar voice.

'Where is she?' I asked.

'Settling into the mares' paddock, over there.' Joe smiled and pointed to a paddock about a hundred metres away, behind the private yards. I could just make out a bright blue fly mask. Honey!

'Can I see her?' I said. 'Just for a minute?'

Joe's mobile phone rang and he pulled it from his trouser pocket. 'I think she'd like that.'

'Cool!' I jogged down the row of yards and found a gate that opened into the paddock. Joe had called it the mares' paddock. I assumed that the Linley mares were kept here together away from the geldings and, if there were any at Linley, the stallions. Knowing how mares could behave when in season I was glad of that. I'd never had any trouble with Honey around Charlie, but they'd known each other for so long they'd probably put any thoughts of a relationship out of their heads. I didn't know if she'd feel the same about other geldings, though, and wasn't keen to find out.

'Honey!' I yelled.

She looked up from the patch of grass she was grazing on. I was glad to see that the grass in the paddock was a lush green. It looked like it had been spelled (rested) for a while. I'd noticed a few empty paddocks — Joe must rotate them every once in a while to give the grass a chance to recover and break the worm cycle. Horses that grazed constantly over manure were always at risk of eating up worm larvae along with their grassy snack. Giving paddocks a good break from horses meant the larvae would die before they could find a nice home for themselves inside a horse.

'Honey!' I called again. She turned her back on me. I slipped through the gate and approached her, calling her name over and over. 'Come over here, will ya?' I said. 'I just want to say hello. I miss you!'

It was true. At home, my bedroom window overlooked Honey's paddock. The kitchen window did too. So even when I wasn't actually with Honey, I was watching her or thinking about her or hearing her. I'd fallen asleep many times to the sound of her gentle grazing. Knowing she was there in her paddock, just a few metres from my bedroom, was comforting. Honey made Shady Creek feel like home to me. I was so glad we'd moved there. I couldn't imagine living in the city any more, having to keep Honey on a farm and seeing her only once a week.

I was only a few steps from her now. She'd gone back to her grazing. Just as I was reaching out for her, a large bay mare with a long nose, a black goggle-eyed fly mask and a bright green rug stepped in front of me. I stepped back, frightened. The only horse Honey had shared a paddock with before was Toffee — apart from those few weeks at Waratah Grove — and Toffee was always too busy chewing his soccer ball to bother me.

'What's with you?' I said to the mare. She snorted and tossed her head. 'Not backing down, eh?'

I reached out to gently push her away. Another horse joined her, black with a white snip on the tip of her nose. Then another. Honey took off towards the corner of the paddock where there was a clump of trees. The mares seemed to be grinning at me, victorious. Then they cantered after Honey, leaving me alone and wondering what had got into my horse.

I let myself out of the gate then made my way back to the boarding house where I changed my shoes. That's when I realized.

I'd stayed too long with Honey.

I was late.

I left my room and stepped out into the Linley courtyard. It was silent. The whole school, the whole universe, was silent. I was alone.

I started to shake. I didn't know what time it was or where to go or what class I had or who was teaching it. I couldn't even remember where I'd left my bag. I reached into my pocket and pulled out my timetable, now a very crumpled piece of paper. I unfolded it and pored over it, sweat forming on my forehead. Was it lesson three or four? Was I supposed to be in Science or History?

I felt so lost, so alone. If only I'd stayed with Em, I thought. Why'd I have to go to see Honey? My eyes started to sting when I remembered that she hadn't wanted to see me anyway.

I folded the paper and pushed it back into my pocket, torn between bursting into tears and running back to my room.

I turned slowly on the spot, hoping to see something or someone, anyone, who'd tell me where to go. I hated Linley, I decided. I'd left Shady Creek and Mum and Dad and Jason and Shady Trails and my job. Becky and Pree were starting together at Shady Creek and Districts High School, where they'd be right now, laughing and talking and having fun and making plans for the weekend. And here I was, lonely and very scared.

'Everything okay?' asked a voice behind me.

I spun around and stared. I opened and closed my mouth a few times but couldn't say anything.

'Lost?' said Mrs Freeman.

I nodded, my mouth hanging open.

She smiled. 'Never mind. Happens to the best of us, especially in the first week. You're just joining us, aren't you?'

I nodded.

'Ashleigh, isn't it? Riding scholarship? I remember you from your interview. I must say I'm looking forward to seeing you ride.'

I nodded again.

Mrs Freeman asked for my timetable and I pulled it out of my pocket, handing it to her.

'Lesson three, History with Mrs Wright. Shall we?'

My throat went all tight and I coughed. 'My bag, I–I've lost … I can't find it.'

'Is that what happened?' Mrs Freeman nodded knowingly. She was so kind. I felt like a creep. I hadn't actually lied to her, but I'd let her think I'd been looking for my bag. 'Not to worry, Ashleigh. They always turn up.'

I followed Mrs Freeman to my class and she knocked on the door. I could see through the glass that the girls were seated in rows at single desks. There was one empty desk in the middle of the third row. The class teacher opened the door and Mrs Freeman ushered me in. The girls saw the principal and sprang to their feet. The teacher stared at me. It was the hat teacher from assembly. I wanted to hide behind Mrs Freeman. I wanted to cling to her and beg her to take me with her. Mrs Freeman introduced me, then left. The door closed behind me and I stood there at the front of the room. Every eye was on me, watching and waiting.

'Welcome, Ashleigh,' the teacher said. 'Mrs Freeman didn't need to introduce you. I've already committed your name to memory. Would you like to know why?'

I swallowed. The hat was gone, but the glare was exactly the same.

'I knew your name because every other girl on my class list managed to arrive on time.' Mrs Wright fixed her laser beam eyes on me. 'Isn't that amazing?'

I'd never met a teacher like Mrs Wright before. I didn't know what to do or say. Staying silent seemed the best policy.

'My classes sit in alphabetical order so you will be directly behind India McCray,' she went on.

I looked up quickly. India was sitting in front of the empty desk. She waved to me brightly.

I walked to my desk, scanning the room for Emily. She wasn't there. As I passed India, she made a faint neighing sound. She knew where I'd been, why I was late.

'Who did that?' Mrs Wright said. 'Who made that noise?'

India raised her hand as I slid into my seat. I was

impressed for a moment by how brave she was, owning up to something like that to someone like Mrs Wright.

'It was Ashleigh,' she said.

'What?' I cried.

'Stand up!' Mrs Wright's face was purple.

I stood, my legs shaking.

Mrs Wright began to rave. About my bad behaviour. About the assembly and answering back and being late and making noises and calling out. I was put on detention and lost ten points for Wilson on my very first day of lessons.

She told me to sit again and I did, my face burning. I didn't hear anything for the rest of the lesson. I just focussed on a small flower carved into the desk. The flower grew more and more hazy until finally, no matter how often I blinked or how hard I rubbed my eyes, it happened. Tears spilled down my face. My first school day at Linley was ruined. All I wanted was to go home.

The bell went, chairs scraped and girls packed up and began to leave. It was time for lesson four: Latin with Mr Finch. I slumped in my seat, waiting for the room to empty. I didn't want anyone to see me like this, especially India.

'You will attend detention for twenty minutes at lunchtime,' Mrs Wright snapped, handing me a piece of paper. 'Really, this has to be some sort of record, Ashleigh. I believe you're the first student I have ever had to punish on the first day of school.'

I looked up, the paper clutched in my hand.

Mrs Wright smoothed her hair. 'Don't let it happen again.'

Then she left.

I dragged myself from the chair and followed my classmates, bagless and alone.

eight

Level B

Finally, it was time for my first riding lesson. 'Thank goodness,' I said to myself as I wriggled into my brand-new bought-for-school joddies and felt the stress of the day fall away. This was what I was here for.

There was a full Linley riding uniform of course, but I didn't have to wear it unless I was competing. I didn't want to, anyway. I wanted to save it. It was so beautiful. Dark navy joddies of the very best quality (white for polocrosse), a light blue polo shirt with the Linley Heights crest embroidered on the front and a plastic sleeve for my competition number sewn into the back. A dark navy helmet with the Linley crest on the front, matching gloves and shiny black knee-high boots. And that was just for gymkhanas and polocrosse. The dressage uniform was breathtaking, but Mum had put her foot down. 'Not unless you're on the team,' she'd said. 'Even then, it'll have to be from Santa. In advance!'

I was at the riding centre in plenty of time. The horses had been rounded up by Joe and were waiting in a large corral, all tied a few metres apart by their lead ropes to pieces of twine. Some were already saddled.

'Honey!' I sighed, wrapping my arms around my horse's neck. I squeezed tight, breathing her in. It was so good to see her. So, so, so good. 'You'll never believe the day I've had.'

As I groomed my horse I filled her in on all the details. She was such a good listener. I knew she understood everything I said to her. Her ears flicked around to wherever I was standing, drinking in the sound of my voice. If I stopped talking, she'd look around to see where I was.

'Can you believe it?' I asked her.

She snorted.

'Obviously not,' I said, laying her saddle blanket on her back. I had a brand-new dark navy Linley Heights saddle blanket for competitions, but I wanted to keep it relatively mud- and horsehair-free (it was the end of Honey's shedding season, but she still managed to cover everything with short copper-coloured hairs!) so I was using my old saddle blanket from home.

I lowered Honey's saddle onto her back as gently as I could. I wouldn't want to have a saddle chucked on me, so I always tried to show my Honey horse the same courtesy.

I walked to her offside and untangled the girth, then walked back to her nearside and threaded one of the two leather straps through the buckle.

Honey tossed her head.

I stopped. She'd never done that before. I pulled up the strap more slowly than before. She tossed her head again, then reached around, teeth bared, making to nip my butt.

I jumped out of the way. 'What's going on?'

Honey tossed her head again. Something was wrong.

'Have you had a bad day too?' I said. 'Those mares giving you a hard time?' I frowned, thinking about the huge bay mare with the goggle-eyed fly mask.

I lifted off the saddle and the saddle blanket and rested them carefully on the corral fence, then ran my hands down Honey's back and around her middle. I didn't take long to find it, under her belly.

'Wow, you've got an ostrich egg!'

I craned my head under her tummy for a close look. The lump was clearly visible, about the same size as a hoof. I ran my hand over it and she flinched.

'I'd say you've copped a kick in the guts,' I groaned. 'No riding today.'

I could have pushed her, I knew. But it wasn't worth it. To put a girth around a sore horse with a huge hoof-shaped haematoma was unfair to her and a big risk to me. Honey was sweet-natured and I knew she loved me as much as I loved her (actually, I think I may have loved her more!), but if she was in pain she'd react instinctively, and her instinct could be to chuck me off — anything to relieve the discomfort.

I waved to Joe, who was saddling a dark, fluffy-maned Welsh Mountain pony. 'She's hurt!'

Joe cast his eye and his hand over the lump. 'It's no good, but it's normal. They're just workin' out the peckin' order. She'll get 'er share of kicks an' bites and dish 'em out in turn.'

'But I can't ride now,' I moaned. 'I mean, I don't want her to suffer and all, but I really, *really* need to ride today.' I gave Joe a look. The same one that always worked on Dad. 'It's my first lesson.'

Joe raised an eyebrow and smiled. 'We 'ave school 'orses, you know. For emergencies.'

'Yes!' I punched the air.

Joe told me to turn Honey out in the mares' paddock again.

'Are you sure?' I said. 'They'll kick her again. Or worse.'

'They 'ave to sort it out eventually.'

I shrugged. 'I guess.'

By the time I got back, there was a cute grey mare standing tacked up where Honey had stood not ten minutes earlier.

'This is Mystery,' said Joe. 'She's yours for today.'

I stroked the mare's sleek neck. She gazed at me with a pair of the gentlest eyes I'd seen. 'She's gorgeous. Thanks.'

Joe patted the mare's shoulder. ''Ave a good lesson. An' try not to worry 'bout your filly. She'll find 'er place in the paddock in no time.'

A bell rang. It was time for my first riding lesson at Linley Heights and I couldn't wait. I untied the twine from Mystery's bridle and led her to the outdoor arena.

★ ★ ★

'Today will just be a chance for me to assess your general riding skills,' our instructor, Demi James, told us as she rode a tall dun gelding at a walk down the line of Year Seven students. She'd already given us a little information about herself (she was a Linley Old Girl who competed at elite level and had returned to teach riding) and had us warm up our horses.

It was strange but exciting to ride a new horse. I missed Honey and the way we connected, but riding a different horse every once in a while was a good way to keep me on my toes. I'd ridden Calypso, my favourite horse at Shady Trails, quite often at work. But that was pleasure riding. Now I was riding raw, having to draw on every skill I'd learnt over the years, every instinct I had about horses. Mystery was a blank page. I knew nothing about her, not even her age, though I guessed that she could be around twelve. I was switched on, concentrating harder than I had in ages. Sometimes riding Honey was so easy, I could forget about the skills, the aids and the rules and just cruise. But not with a new horse. I had to stay alert, focussed. I had to really ride.

I glanced down the line of riders. I didn't recognize anyone, especially in their helmets. Only India, on her chestnut, just a few horses down from me, was familiar. I didn't like India — the way she'd known my name; the way she'd got me into trouble on purpose. I could feel her watching me. I knew she was checking me out, making her own assessment of my general riding skills. I knew she'd memorized the riding scholarship criteria and was weighing me up against it. I had two people to impress in the arena that day.

'We're warmed up, so the horses should be limber. I shouldn't need to point out to any of you the critical importance of warming up a horse before exercise,' Demi said. 'None of you would want to be dragged out of bed first thing in the morning and made to run a cross-country course while somebody sat on your back thrashing you with a whip to make you go faster. Horses feel pretty much the same way.'

I was sure Mystery was ready for anything. Our fifteen-minute warm-up had included walking, trotting and cantering in both directions, making sure she worked both sides of her body. So far, she was a pleasure to ride. Her steps were even. She was forward, willing and fit. She moved into her paces at the slightest pressure from my lower legs. She was on the bit, responsive to my hands, and I felt totally safe on her back.

'I've planned out a series of simple exercises to help me grade you into levels,' Demi said. 'The level you're placed in now won't be set in stone, but it'll make training, competing and advancing easier.'

A girl on my left raised her hand.

'Sally?' Demi said.

'Can we go up a level?' Sally asked.

Some other riders murmured. From the sounds of it, Sally wasn't alone in wondering that.

Demi smiled. 'Absolutely. I did say they're not set in stone. At the beginning I'd prefer to be cautious and grade you conservatively. For your safety as well as your horse's. But if I feel you should be riding at a more advanced level, I'll certainly move you up a grade or two.'

'Yes!' Sally said, clearly pleased with Demi's response.

'Time to begin. I'd like everyone to move into a walk, clockwise around the arena. Make sure you give yourselves, and each other, plenty of space. Please remember arena etiquette. If you're a slower rider, you should always take the inside track; faster riders take the outside track.'

I fell into place behind a small girl on a huge mare that looked to be at least 15 hands high. I was impressed by and terrified for her at the same time.

'When passing riders going in the opposite direction, you should always pass right shoulder to right shoulder,' Demi continued. 'Anyone out of control or who deliberately disobeys me or the arena rules will be asked to dismount and leave the arena immediately. Stay at a walk, lower legs in light contact with your horse's sides, hands keeping an even pressure on the reins. India — look up, look ahead! You don't have to stare at your horse's head like that. It's not going to fall off!'

I giggled.

'On the count of five we're moving to a rising trot — one, two — Ebony, take a breath. You haven't breathed in since you mounted. You're turning blue! Three, four, five, rising trot!'

I squeezed my calves against Mystery's sides, asking for the trot. She responded at once.

'Ask, insist, demand!' Demi called. 'If your horse hasn't responded to your ask, you must apply more pressure and move to the insist. If they still don't respond, apply more pressure! The demand.'

Some girls moved to the inside track, a few metres to the right, because their horses refused to trot or because they didn't feel comfortable trotting. The inside track is like a slow lane, which allows horses working at a quicker pace to continue in the other lane without any accidents. The rules are the same in every arena; it's like a universal code.

'You there, with the pink joddies!' Demi called.

'Natalia,' the girl said.

'Use your dummy spurs on him, let him know they're there. But be light with them. We don't want him jumping to the moon if you jab him.'

Within a few moments Natalia's horse had moved into a trot.

'Now only use your spurs when you need to remind him to keep trotting,' Demi said. 'Too much spurring can desensitize a horse to leg aids.'

Demi kept riding around at a walk, watching every rider keenly. I liked her. She reminded me of Holly, my first-ever riding teacher who'd never let her students put anything less than a hundred and fifty per cent into their riding. The care of their horses too.

'Nice trot, ladies. Good. Hang on — you on the Appaloosa. What are you doing flapping your legs around like that? Gentle, controlled pressure is all she needs. She's not a bucking bronco! Better. Much better!'

I looked straight ahead, concentrating on my rising trot, feeling confident that I was riding well.

'You, there on the grey!' Demi called.

I leaned forward just slightly, making sure I wasn't rising too high in the saddle. I could hear Mystery's two-beat pace, could feel her springing from one diagonal pair of legs to the other.

'Who is that girl? Someone tell me her name!'

'Her name's Ashleigh,' someone said.

'Ashleigh!' Demi called. 'Hello! Ashleigh on the grey!'

I used my outside leg to urge Mystery onto the now empty inside track, closed my legs on her ribs, just behind her girth, stretched down with my heels and sat deep in the saddle, closing my fingers around the reins. Mystery slowed to a halt.

'Me?' I looked around.

Demi was waving to me, a stern look on her face. 'Yes, you. You're on a grey. Why didn't you respond straightaway?'

I was confused. 'A grey? She's a chestnut.'

The other riders broke up laughing.

'Concentrate!' Demi snapped. The laughter stopped.

'I'm sorry,' I said. 'I forgot I was on a school horse. My horse, my chestnut, she's injured. I've had to rest her. I didn't realize you meant me, otherwise I would have—'

'Don't worry about it,' Demi said, holding up her hand in the 'stop' signal. 'Just pay more attention to who you're riding next time.'

'Yes, Miss.'

'It's Demi.'

'Yes, Miss Demi.'

Demi smiled. 'Just Demi. This is riding, not History!'

'Thank goodness!' I said.

Demi raised an eyebrow. 'You were riding on the wrong diagonal. I was watching you for a while, and while your technique is lovely you—'

'Wrong diagonal?'

'Yeah.' Demi stretched her legs in the saddle. 'Riders, change direction! The trot is a diagonal two-beat pace in which the near foreleg and off hind leg and the off foreleg and near hind leg touch the ground at the same time, yes?'

I nodded. 'Yes.'

'There's also a moment of suspension when all four feet are off the ground at the same time, yes?'

I nodded again.

'Okay. When we're riding in an arena we're usually riding in circles. Big, small, whatever, we ride in circles a *lot*.'

'True,' I said. My ears were straining. I wanted to remember every word she said. No one had ever taught me like this before and I wanted to make the most of it.

'A rider can ride on the right diagonal or the left diagonal.'

'I'm getting lost,' I said.

'Diagonal, as in diagonal pairs of legs, remember?'

'Yes.' I rubbed Mystery's mane to let her know I was pleased with her.

Demi twisted around in her saddle and called to the others. 'On the count of five you're going to ask for a canter! One, two — when you're riding in a circle the rider should be sitting on the outside diagonal — three, four — meaning that the outside front and inside hind legs of the horse will be in the air when the rider is out of the saddle — five!'

The riders moved to a canter. Even Natalia.

'To ride on the correct diagonal you should be in the saddle when your horse's feet are on the ground and rise out of the saddle when the horse's feet are off the ground. It helps the horse to engage its hindquarters properly. And we all know the hindquarters are the powerhouse.'

'How about when you change direction?' I said. 'What happens then?'

'Simple, you do exactly the same thing. Want to give it a try?'

I nodded. 'Definitely.'

'Inside track, please, trot when you're ready. Go!' Demi moved her dun out of my way. 'Riders, change direction! Ashleigh, you're on the wrong diagonal.'

I muttered at myself, unable to believe I'd been through all this training and not learnt something so basic. I was a graduate of Waratah Grove and here I was getting my trot polished up at Linley Heights.

'Sit down for one rising movement then rise again on the correct diagonal. Wrong!'

I muttered some more.

'Tell yourself, down, down, up! It usually works.'

'Down, down, up,' I said to myself, rising out of the saddle.

'Wrong! Down, down, up!' Demi called. 'Riders, slow to a trot, please.'

'Down, down, up,' I said. 'Down, down, up.' I sat for two paces and rose again.

'Good girl!' Demi shouted. 'Terrific. Can you feel that?'

'Yeah,' I said, smiling. 'I can.'

'Keep it up, don't change what you're doing. Keep it up for five minutes. Hold your reins in your right hand and put your left on her rump. Can you feel it going up and down?'

'Yes.'

'She's up, you're up. She's down, you're down. Get it?'

I got it. And I loved Demi's lesson.

By the time we were cooling out our horses we'd been graded into our levels, from A to D. India was the only rider to make it to A level. I was a B. Sally was a C and Natalia was a D. Most riders were C level.

'Nice riding, Ashleigh,' India said as we walked our horses from the arena. 'You must be so embarrassed. I think you're the first riding scholarship recipient ever to be placed in B level. But you won't have to worry about all that pressure to perform when you're stripped of your entitlements. You can go back to whatever little rock you crawled out from under and forget all about Linley.'

'What's your problem?' I said, holding so tight to Mystery's reins I thought I might snap them in two. 'What've I done to you? I don't even know you.'

India stopped her horse and looked into my eyes. 'I want that scholarship. And I'm gonna make sure I get it. So just keep riding the way you did today. And that detention'll work wonders as well. You'll see — by the end of this term you'll be back where you belong and I'll be the Year Seven riding scholarship recipient, the way it should have been in the first place.'

Anger surged through me. 'Why don't you just—'

'Awesome riding today, Ashleigh.'

I turned around. It was Demi, the only person in the arena whose opinion actually mattered.

'And on a new horse as well. That's the real test of a rider's skills. It's so easy to get lazy on a familiar horse. You get to that point where you know the horse so well you go on autopilot.' Demi led her dun gelding in the opposite direction to India and me. 'Keep it up, Ashleigh. I'm sure you'll be moved to A level by the end of term.'

I grinned at India. 'I s'pose it was easy for you to be placed in A level on autopilot on a familiar horse.'

India's eyes narrowed and she sucked in her breath. 'You—'

'See ya!' I sang, leading Mystery away. I was totally buzzed. To end such a rotten day this way was the best. Better than the best.

I untacked, hosed, rubbed down, groomed and rugged Mystery, then returned her to Joe who turned her out in the school paddock for her afternoon biscuit of lucerne hay. We stood side by side, watching Mystery eat.

'How'd it go?' he said.

'It was unreal.'

What else could I say? There were no other words.

'So, how do you like Linley so far?' he asked.

I thought about that. I thought about Claire and India and Mrs Wright. I thought about being away from home and missing Mum, Dad and Jason. I thought about Becky and Pree and Jenna. I even thought about detention.

Then I thought about riding.

'I love it.'

I meant every one of those three little words.

nine

Ricki the Remarkable

'So how was it?' Emily asked after breakfast. We were in the library, queuing up for our textbooks. I had to pick up textbooks for Maths, Science, History, Geography, Art, Latin, French, Music, Drama, Design and Technology, and Horsemanship. Then there was a book of poetry, another textbook and a novel for English, plus a dictionary, a set of geometry instruments and a calculator.

'The best ever,' I said. 'So amazing, so awesome, so—'

'I get it,' Em said sourly.

'Talk to your mum. Surely she'd let you have a few riding lessons if she knew how much it means to you.'

I felt so sorry for Emily. Her parents were forcing her to be someone she didn't want to be. Banning her from following her dream. I couldn't understand how she put up with it. I'd always wanted the horsy life. I wouldn't have settled for anything else.

'You don't know my mum.' Emily sighed and pulled out her textbook list. 'Can you believe how much stuff we have to collect?'

'No,' I said. 'We need a donkey to cart all this back to our rooms. Speaking of donkeys—'

'Don't mention India McCray,' Emily said. 'I just had breakfast. You don't wanna wear my scrambled eggs, do you?' She put her hand over her mouth.

I shook my head. 'How did we get on to egg sandwiches? I was talking about riding. I promised to teach you to ride and I will. Honey needs a week off to get that lump down, but I rode the most gorgeous horse yesterday. I'll ask Joe if I can ride her again and then you can have a go. She won't hurt you. Your mum'll never know.'

'Shh!' Em looked terrified. 'The walls have ears here. Just like big sisters.'

I rolled my eyes and shuffled forward in the queue. I didn't get it. If I were Em, I wouldn't care what my mum said. I'd just do it. Maybe.

'Can I trouble you for just a moment?' said a voice behind me.

I looked over my right shoulder. There was nobody there.

'Excuse me, Miss.'

I looked over my left. There was no one on that side either.

'I seem to have lost my gold coin,' said the voice.

I jumped around this time and came face to face with a pretty girl with a wild mass of dark, almost waist-long, very curly hair, a dimple on one side of her face, eyes so dark they were almost black and braces on her teeth.

'Oh my stars! I've found it. Right here behind your ear!'

The girl reached forward and pulled a gold coin from behind my ear then held it up in the air. The queue of students clapped.

'Now, for my next trick, I will make this queue disappear!' The girl waved her arms around. 'Abracababra!'

'Isn't that "abracadabra"?' I said.

'There are no rules in magic, only …' The girl did a spin. 'Wonder! Abracandelabra!'

She reached into the pocket of her tunic, pulled out her closed fist, then blew into it. Silver sparkles flew into the air, landing on much of the queue.

'I've gotta work on that one,' the girl said.

'Ricki Samuels!'

The girl brushed off her hands frantically and turned to me. 'Let me in front of you? Please?'

I nodded. 'No worries.'

Ricki squeezed into line and pushed her hands into the pockets of her tunic, whistled and stared up at the ceiling.

A librarian appeared, almost by magic herself. 'How many times have I told you not to clown around in my library?'

Ricki gazed up at her, a picture of innocence. 'Moi?'

'Oh yes, you,' said the librarian.

I peered at her identity tag: *Mrs Edwina Curry, Head Librarian*.

'In the interests of student safety and my sanity, please restrict your performances to the playground,' she said.

I was sure there was a hint of a smile on Mrs Curry's face. But only a small hint. She walked away, glancing over her shoulder for a moment, then disappeared into what seemed to be a textbook storeroom.

Ricki grabbed my hand, pumping it up and down. 'Thanks for that, mate. I owe ya one! Oh my stars — you've taken my gold coin again. Here it is, right in your hand!'

She peeled my hand open and there was her coin. I giggled.

'Ricki Samuels,' she said. 'Otherwise known as …' She made a dramatic sweeping movement with her arm, as if she was unfurling some wonderful, although completely invisible cloak. '… Ricki the Remarkable!'

'I'm Ashleigh,' I said. 'Ashleigh Miller. But my mates call me Ash. And this is Emily.'

Em introduced herself and shook hands with Ricki.

'You know this one?' Ricki did the most complicated handshake I'd ever seen with Em. 'Remember that and we'll do it every time we see each other.' She pointed at me. 'You too.'

'Are you new?' I said, taking a few steps forward in the queue.

Ricki shook her head. 'Been here since kindy.'

Em nudged my side and I smiled. Finally we'd found a friendly since-kindyer!

'I'm a day girl,' she went on. 'I live right here in town. You guys are boarders, right?'

Em and I nodded and told her where we'd come from.

'I don't know how you do it. I could never board. I'd miss my mum's cooking too much. She is the *best*.' Ricki's dark eyes were wide.

'Look, Madison, it's Icki!'

India McCray stopped in front of the three of us with a girl I didn't know who was all blonde, pink and soft-looking with watery blue eyes and a nose so turned up I could see right into her nostrils.

'Hey, India,' Ricki said. 'What's up?'

India smiled. 'Nothing's up. Specially not you. Remember that fall she took, Madds? What a classic, eh? Couldn't ride a rocking horse, could she?'

Ricki yawned hugely, patting her open mouth with her hand. 'That was three years ago, Indy. Can't you think of something new?'

'No.' India laughed. Her friend laughed too. 'Oh, hi, Ashleigh! How's Level B? Make sure you stay away from the horses, Amelia.'

With that, they muscled their way into the queue in front of the girl I'd seen crying in the dining hall on our first day at Linley Heights.

'It's Emily!' Em's face reddened. 'I can't stand her. And I've only known her for four days.'

Ricki grinned. 'Try seven years. But don't worry. I've been working on this trick, see. All I need is a cane toad willing to switch bodies with her. And someone willing to kiss her once it's actually done.'

'You wouldn't have much luck convincing anyone except another cane toad,' I grumbled.

Ricki laughed. 'Good one! Hey, check this out. Watch as I pull an ordinary pink hanky from my pocket.'

Ricki held up a pink satin hanky for everyone to see, then poked it into her closed fist. 'I just say the magic word — *ubalabubbala*! And now you see right before your eyes …'

She pulled the hanky out again grandly. 'Oh.'

Em squinted at the hanky from behind her glasses. 'Isn't that the exact same—'

Ricki coughed. 'Never mind. I just need a bit more practice to get that one perfectly right. At least the queue's disappeared.' She pushed the hanky into the pocket of her tunic and beamed at us.

'Ten minutes after you tried to vanish it,' I pointed out. 'I don't think that counts.'

'Patience, Ash, my friend. Magic is all about patience.'

Em folded her arms. 'I thought it was all about the hand being quicker than the eye.'

Ricki winked. 'It's about that too.'

'Do you still ride?' I asked, reading over my list again.

Ricki shook her head. 'Sometimes. Not as much since that fall India was going on about.'

'But everyone knows that if you fall off a horse you should get straight back on.' I was amazed that a Linley girl wouldn't know such a basic equestrian fact.

'I could be tempted to return to the saddle if I could just find my gold coin,' Ricki said, grinning. 'I know I left it here somewhere.'

She tiptoed up behind India. The girls watching her giggled.

'India?' Ricki said, tapping her on the shoulder.

'What d'you want, freak?' India's face suggested she'd just smelt something terrible.

'It's my gold coin. You seem to be hiding it *up your nose!*'

Ricki made a flashy move with her right hand and appeared to pull her coin from India's left nostril. She wiped it on her uniform and held it up high for everyone to see.

'Make sure that's a coin!' I gasped between whoops of laughter.

'Who knows what else she's got up there?' Emily was hysterical.

'And now for my next trick, I will make myself disappear!' Ricki cried. 'Oobooladooboo!'

She threw a handful of magic glitter in the air and ran, just as Mrs Curry made her second appearance at the door of the storeroom.

'Ricki Davis!' she cried, red-faced. But Ricki was gone.

Em and I high-fived. We'd found a new mate at Linley. Ricki was just what we needed.

That afternoon I went to the riding centre alone. Em had to start on an English project, and I wanted to spend some quiet time with Honey and check her lump.

I caught her and led her to her stall, talking to her quietly about my day. Every horse had its own stall at Linley Heights School. It was for grooming, feeding and just spending time in. It would be especially handy in bad weather, hot or wet.

I fixed a haynet to the wall and let Honey tear at it for a while. Once she was content I set about brushing her. This groom wasn't about how she looked. It was about bonding, about just being with her. Mum did the same kind of thing with Jason. She'd lie him in her lap and run a soft-bristled brush over his almost-bald head or tickle his toes. And he'd gurgle and look up into her face like she was the most fascinating thing in the entire world (let's face it, she was — in his world) and it was so special I'd feel like crying. This was the horsy equivalent for me. I'd just brush and brush and stroke Honey and tell her all my thoughts and the secrets I could never tell anyone else.

'Talking to your horse?'

'Who doesn't?' I said.

India McCray was leaning on Honey's stall, watching me. She had on her green and yellow jacket even though it was February-hot. I was starting to suspect she liked to be seen in it.

'Better watch what you say to her,' she said. 'And to me.'

'India, I've got better things to do right now than talk to you, so if you could go find the nearest bag of manure and stick your head in it, that'd be great. Thanks.'

I turned my back on her and worked on picking some dry grass out of Honey's tail.

'I just came to warn you. About Ricki.'

I didn't want to continue the conversation, but she'd reeled me in with that one. 'What about her?'

'If you know what's good for you, you'll stay away from her.'

I shook Honey's tail and tried to run a brush through it. Knotty. Needed the detangling spray. With every horse tail hair taking at least a year to grow, I didn't want to be pulling any out.

'Why?' I said, fishing around in my grooming kit for the spray. The kit was packed with all of Honey's beauty requirements — elastic bands and tins of hoof oil and a jar of petroleum jelly for shining up her face. There was even horse fly spray. I pulled out the detangler.

'She's weird,' India sneered. 'You saw what she's like. We were actually friends, years ago. She used to be all right until that fall she had and then she went all strange and started doing those dumb tricks all the time.'

'So?' I said. 'What difference does it make to you?'

I sprayed Honey's tail, set down my bottle and ran my comb straight through it. 'That's better.'

'I just don't wanna see you get hurt. You know, by the other girls. Ricki doesn't have any friends after seven years at Linley. Don't you think that's a sign?'

I sighed. 'It's a sign, all right. It's a sign of you telling new people to stay away from her. What did she do to you, anyway?'

I was proud of myself. The old me would have backed into a corner and shaken with fear. The new Linley me was sticking up for myself, and for my new friend. India McCray didn't scare me at all. But she was annoying me a whole lot.

India's green eyes flashed. 'She's just whacko, that's all. I'm only telling you this to be nice.'

I took my sponge and lifted Honey's tail, cleaning under her dock. 'No, you're not. You're serving me up a huge plate of this.' I pointed to the pile of poo Honey had deposited while I was rummaging in my kit.

'I'm giving you a chance,' India said. 'Be my friend and ditch those losers. We can ride together. We'd be unstoppable as a team. You'll be better off in the end, I promise you.'

I set my sponge down and took a step towards India.

'I wouldn't be your friend if you were the last girl in the school. And I'll never ride with you.'

Her eyes narrowed. 'Have it your way. But this was my only offer. Anything that happens from now on is your own doing.'

I folded my arms and smiled. 'Bring it on.'

India marched away, past the other stalls. 'Remember, it's your own fault!' she yelled.

I shook my head. India almost gave Carly the Creep a run for her money.

I tried to concentrate on Honey but it was almost impossible. There had to be a reason India had come to me about Ricki. I had to find out what it was.

ten

Rules of the Game

'Ever played polocrosse before?' Maryanne James said.

She stood with me in the centre of the Linley polocrosse field swinging a long-handled, loose-netted racquet in one hand and balancing what looked like a miniature rubber netball in the other. It was my first-ever training session.

'Never,' I said. 'But I really wanna learn.'

'You really have to learn. You're on the team automatically, remember?'

I nodded.

'Okay,' Maryanne began. 'There's a lot to take in and if you don't understand, stop me. Got it?'

I nodded again. 'Got it.'

'Polocrosse is an awesome sport. It's a combination of polo, lacrosse and netball.'

'Sounds like a salad!'

Maryanne smiled. 'Never thought of it that way. Anyway, there are six players per team. The six get split into two groups of three who play alternate chukkas.'

'Chukkas?'

'A chukka is a period of time in the game. A maximum of eight minutes to be exact.'

'Chukka — eight minutes — six players — got it.'

'Good. So, your first three play the first chukka, then your second three play the next chukka and so on. There are usually six to eight chukkas per game, depending on the age of the players.' Maryanne threw the ball into the air and caught it in her racquet.

'Okay.' I slotted the information into the relevant folder in my brain. There's a finite amount of space in there so a good storage system is very important.

'Each player has a position and job on the field. Number One is attack, Number Two is the centre and Number Three is defence.'

'So that's the netball part,' I said, understanding a little.

'Right. Player Number One is the only player allowed to score, okay?'

I nodded. 'Okay.'

'Look at the field,' Maryanne said, sweeping her arm around.

I looked. The field was grassed with white lines painted on it like a football field. But the markings were similar to a netball court. There were two goalposts at either end, and a semicircle painted in front of each set. A few metres after the semicircle was a long line painted right across the field at either end. A large clear middle section separated the two.

'See those goalposts?' Maryanne said. 'The area in front of them is the goal-scoring area. Number One is only allowed to score from there. The Number Three player will be there as well, defending the goal.'

'Got it,' I said. 'But what about Number Two?'

'Number Two is the centre, right? So she's only allowed to play in the centre area.'

I stared at the field. 'Where's that?'

'That larger section between the two goal-scoring areas.'

'Is there a referee?'

'No, an umpire. But there can be a ref — only in games where there are two umpires, though. The ref is there to make a final decision.'

'Like a video ref?'

'Right!'

'Is the ump on horseback?'

Maryanne nodded. 'You bet, and they wear these black and white shirts, a bit like a chessboard. There are goal umpires, line umpires, timekeepers and scorers as well. Ready for more?'

I gave her the thumbs up. 'I'm ready.'

'The game starts in the centre. The players all line up and the umpy chucks the ball in. The players try to catch the ball and if they don't they can pick it up off the ground.'

'With their hands?' I said, thinking about all those Riding Club mounted games I'd played.

'No way,' Maryanne said. 'With the racquet. It's also called "the stick" by the way.'

'What happens when someone gets the ball?'

She shrugged. 'Easy. They throw it from player to player until Number One has it and can throw a goal.'

'From the goal-scoring area only, right?'

Maryanne smiled. 'Right. You're a quick learner.'

'But how does the other team get the ball? It's not like you can tackle or anything.'

'Definitely not. The ball can be dropped, which gives the other team a chance, or intercepted in midair. Players can also hit the other team's sticks, to get the ball out. But you can only hit up, never down. And never hit a horse with the stick. Anything like that just hands the other team a penalty. Oh, and don't wave your stick around like a loony.'

'How am I s'posed to ride with something like that in my hand?' I pointed at Maryanne's racquet.

'You hold both reins in your left hand and the stick in your right. The horse's offside is called the stick side in polocrosse.'

'Stick side, got it.'

Maryanne raised one eyebrow. 'You sure?'

I winked. 'Totally sure.'

'You'll have to read the rule book later, and you'll pick up lots in training. And if you have any questions, ask me, or any of the other girls. There's one other Year Seven playing polocrosse — India McCray. I'm sure she'll be glad to help you.'

I coughed, despite my best efforts to do nothing but smile.

'Oh, and before I forget, never ride through the goalposts!' Maryanne said. 'There's a goal umpire standing there who doesn't feel like becoming a pancake.'

I giggled. 'I won't.'

'Throwing and catching practice now.' Maryanne handed me the racquet.

The stick looked like it was made from cane and was quite light. It had to have been at least a metre long. The head was shaped a bit like a squash racquet, with a tough, shallow net bag where the tight crossed strings should have been. The handle of the stick was bandaged for grip. I swung it about, getting a feel for it, getting used to its weight and length. I tried to imagine riding around with it in my hand for eight minutes at a time and shuddered.

'I'll throw you the ball,' Maryanne said. 'You catch it and then throw it back to me. But with the stick, okay?'

'No worries,' I said. 'Give me the best you've got.'

She did. I missed many more balls than I caught. And most of my throws became tangled in the net. I was glad there was still weeks to go until the first in-school match.

We stopped after what seemed like hours. I was

sweaty and exhausted, but pumped. It was going to be fun. I was a mounted games rider. I'd always got my kicks from riding fast with my team to win. I couldn't wait to get on the field. My only concern was Honey. She may have played or she may never have seen a polocrosse field before. There was no way for me to know. I'd just have to get out there and give it a try, see what she could and couldn't do and take it from there.

'Don't tell me, it was brilliant, right?' Em was snuggled up in the comfiest single-seater lounge chair in the boarders' lounge, wearing her pyjamas and fluffy purple slippers with a pale blue Linley towel wrapped around her head like a turban.

'Sure was,' I said, grinning. 'Did you know that polocrosse is one of only three truly Australian sports?'

'Uh-huh.'

'And that the Hirsts formed the first polocrosse club ever in Australia in 1939?'

'I did know that, actually. Most likely because you've already told me on several occasions.' Em snatched at the TV remote control. 'Now shush about horses for at least half an hour. I wanna watch TV.'

'Don't you wanna know what the other two sports are?' I poked at Em's foot with mine. I'd left my slippers at home so I had to make do with my thongs. I'd been writing a list of all the things I'd forgotten to bring to school so that when I went home on my first exeat weekend, in three weeks' time, I'd remember to bring them back with me. 'AFL and camp-drafting, and camp-drafting is—'

'Another horse sport. Ash, do you have an off switch?' Em pointed the remote at me and pressed some buttons.

'They don't work on me. Mum and Dad have tried everything. Not even the garage-door remote makes a difference. Wanna play ping-pong?'

Emily frowned. 'No. I already told you, I want to see my show. Besides, for once there's no one fighting over the TV. It's a sign!'

I craned my neck over the lounge to see what the other girls were up to. It was unusual not to have a crowd around the TV after prep (homework and study period) was over. The boarders' lounge was huge and separated into different sections by dividing walls. There was the TV area, a games room with computers (we used them for emailing as well) and games consoles available to play with. There was a reading room where a stack of library books were kept and changed every few weeks so there were always new books to read. There was a section with a ping-pong table and pinball machines. There was also a kitchen where we could keep snacks and drinks and make ourselves a late-night bowl of cereal or slice of toast. Next to that was a laundry with washing machines, dryers and ironing boards (we could use the school laundry service but there were always emergencies!). There was also a quiet room where you could just curl up on a lounge and talk.

'They're all squeezed into the reading room,' I said.

Emily grunted. 'That'll make Claire happy.'

'She does spend a lot of time in there, doesn't she. It's odd, really. With all those germy books.'

'Hmm.' Em was watching her show, mesmerized by a cute guy with glaringly white teeth.

'Think I'll go check it out,' I said.

'Hmm.'

I waved my hand in front of Em's face. She didn't flinch.

I left her to Tooth Guy and wandered over to the reading room. Claire was standing on a chair speaking to the boarders. There were no doors on any of the rooms so it was easy to hear what she was saying.

'I've had enough,' she said. 'And I'd be amazed if some of you haven't too. It's time to do something before one of us is injured, killed or gets some kind of disgusting disease.'

'What are you talking about?' I said, squeezing my way into the room.

'Horse riding program,' said a Year Nine boarder with a long plait. 'She's trying to get it closed down.'

'What?' I gasped. Claire had said as much a few times, but I'd never really thought she was serious. 'Do you agree with her?'

The girl shrugged. 'I couldn't care less. I'm not here for the horses.'

'But I am,' I said, anger bubbling up inside me. 'Why don't you just shut up, Claire?'

The room fell silent at once, as if someone had switched off some noisy machine. Some of the girls laughed. A few 'oohed'.

'Hey, new girl,' a tall girl said. 'I don't remember anyone ringing your bell.'

Claire smiled. 'My mother, as you all know, is president of the Parents' Association and she's organized a meeting for students and parents about this horse problem for the Friday before the first weekend exeat. That gives all of your parents a chance to let Mrs Freeman know their real feelings when they come to pick you up.'

'You can't do this!' I yelled. 'It's not fair.'

'It's not fair for me either,' Claire snapped, 'being stuck with those filthy things every year for seven years.'

'But you never go anywhere near the horses. How can they hurt you?'

'People like you bring the dirt back to the boarding house. You have hair on your clothes and horse mess on your shoes and bacteria on your hands and you touch everything!' Claire was breathing hard. It seemed that even thinking about the germs was too much for her.

'That's crazy!' I said. My whole body was cold and I felt sick. It looked like Claire wasn't the only one who had a problem with the horses. If these girls got their way, there was no point in my being at Linley at all.

The room emptied and Claire and I stood face to face.

'I'm not gonna let you do this,' I said.

Claire rolled her eyes. 'Oh, please. Who's Mrs Freeman going to listen to? I've been here since kindy. My mum and her mum are Old Girls. My mum's the president of the Parents' Association. My grandmother was school captain. We pay fees. Why would she listen to someone who's been here a week and comes here for free?'

I reached out to Claire, to grab her arm or something. I don't know, really. She pushed my hand away.

'Don't touch me!'

And she stormed out, leaving me in the room alone.

I wasn't going to let this happen. New or not, I was never going to let this happen. I rushed back to Emily. We had to make plans. Fast.

eleven

By a Nose

'I'm so glad you're okay now,' I told Honey as I prepared her for our first in-school funkhana (a gymkhana that's not so serious, just for fun). It was a week after Claire's big announcement and I was glad of the distraction. I'd been totally stressed, worrying about the meeting, counter-action planning with Em and Ricki, trying to find my way around, get to all my classes on time and do all my homework. I hadn't had even one email back from Becky. Or a call for that matter. Not even a text. My violin and I weren't getting along well at all. Even the teacher winced when I played (tortured) it. The funkhana was just what I needed.

I was dressed for the first time in my Linley riding uniform and I felt fantastic. Mum had made me buy it two sizes too big, to 'grow into', so it probably didn't look as fantastic as it could have. But I was so excited and so looking forward to riding Honey in front of much of the school that I didn't care.

Honey had been shampooed, groomed, sprayed with glossy stuff, plaited, quarter-marked (then hairsprayed) and had her nails done so she was looking like a squillion bucks. I'd spent hours cleaning my tack as well, so I was dying for a shot at the Tack and Turnout class where Honey would be judged on how well groomed she was and how well presented her tack was. As I led her out into the marshalling area of the Linley outdoor arena, I was prouder than I'd ever been.

India was already there on her chestnut, Rusty, along with Natalia from my riding class on Rosie, Sally on Mack, and lots of other, bigger girls. It seemed that no one who did riding wanted to miss out. And it was a closed weekend, which meant that no boarder was allowed to go off campus, so we had a ready-made (trapped!) audience.

I'd signed up for lots of mounted games, some individual and some team. At this funkhana, riders were simply split into two groups — riders under fifteen years and riders fifteen years and over — which meant I'd be competing with and against girls in Years Eight and Nine at the very least. I'd never been up against riders who were that much older than me. Part of me felt scared. After all, if they'd been alive two years longer than me they had two years more riding experience — a slight advantage for them. But another part of me, the more sensible part, was happy. Mounted games were a great way of developing my riding skills, especially when I was thrown against older, better riders. I'd have to dig extra deep if I was going to stand a chance against them. I'd had heaps of mounted games experience, but Shady Creek Riding Club was small. At Linley, there were so many riders I was practically tripping over them.

The first classes were the presentation classes. It was enter on the day (for free — yay!) so Honey and I competed in Led Galloway Mare (a class for horses from 14 hands high to 15 hands high) where I simply led Honey around the arena and she was judged on her conformation: how well built she was (we came second); Tack and Turnout (we came third); and Pair of Galloways (I teamed up with a Year Nine girl called Caroline and her gelding, Rupert, for a win!).

Next were the mounted games. I was all bubbly inside. I'd been dying for a chance to ride hard and fast and, hopefully, win a few ribbons. This funkhana didn't count towards the end-of-year Linley Cup so I wanted to simply enjoy it. And I wasn't going to knock back any opportunity to show India exactly what she was up against.

There was a half-hour break to give us time to tack up and warm up our horses. I wasted no time in getting to the indoor arena where the warm-ups were being done. It was busy inside, but Honey and I slipped into the stream of horses and riders and spent twenty minutes moving around and around in both directions at the walk, trot and canter. By the time we left, Honey was warm and starting to sweat. This was what we both wanted. Only a completely ignorant rider would ever ride her horse in mounted games without warming it up first. That was a recipe for injury.

The first games were individual. We were separated into heats of six riders under or over fifteen years of age. First and second in any heat would go on to compete for places in the event. The first game was Stepping Stones — I had to race Honey to a series of ten upside-down buckets all joined together with rope (the stepping stones), dismount, run along the stepping stones without falling off (if I did, I'd have to go back to the beginning), remount and race to the finish. There were four heats; I was put into the second. The first heat lined up and the starter (a senior girl) raised the bell.

On the bell, the riders burst from the starting line. I noticed something straightaway: most of them did flying dismounts (dismounting while the horse is still moving to save time). I'd done flying dismounts when I had to on my school horse, Princess, back in the city. But I'd never tried it on Honey. There was a simple reason for this. Princess was about 13 hands high, while Honey was 14 hands high. That ten centimetres made a big difference — while I was this tall, anyway. (I hadn't grown a whole lot since then, that was for sure.) I supposed I could have a go. The worst that could happen was I'd fall and be mangled by her churning legs. The best that could happen was I'd save time and face in front of India, who was standing in the third-heat group behind me, still in her jacket (second skin, more like!), sending a laser beam glare into the back of my helmet. Yes, I thought, I'll definitely have to do a flying dismount. But a vault (mounting while the horse is moving) after I'd completed the stepping stones would be impossible.

The first heat was finished and two girls had made it to the final round. The marshal, a riding instructor for the older girls, yelled and waved and my heat moved to the starting line.

I stopped Honey on the line and clung to my reins. This was only a game. It was only for fun. But I had something to prove. Again. I'd never felt this way in the city, at South Beach Stables. But it kept happening over and over since then: at Shady Creek Riding Club, at Waratah Grove, and now at Linley Heights. It seemed that everywhere I rode now I had to prove my worth to someone. Or was it just to myself? Whichever, the stress of it could sometimes dull the glow of riding for me. I wasn't going to let that happen this time, I decided. Today I was going to fly!

The starter raised her hand and I raised mine on the reins. Honey tensed her body and danced on her forelegs. I knew the speed was coming and I couldn't wait. I needed it. Like I needed oxygen.

The bell rang.

Honey knew exactly what I wanted her to do. My eyes were fixed on the stepping stones and with a mere touch from my legs Honey exploded into a canter. It was only a few moments, just a few beats of our hearts, until the buckets were close enough for me to kick my feet from the stirrups. I bore my weight down and straightened up, closing my legs in on Honey's ribs. When she'd slowed to a trot I leaned forward so far my face was close to her neck. I flipped my legs back and up and then over, and I was airborne beside her. I hit the ground running and held tight to her reins. She stayed at the trot. I reached the first stone, a bright blue plastic bucket, and stepped on, careful not to overbalance. I looked to my right quickly. There was no one there. On my left I could just make out a grey pony. I took each stepping stone at a jog, eight, nine, then ten. Now I was in for it. The grey pony was small, maybe only 12 hands, and very easy to vault back onto. I, on the other hand, had to bring Honey to a complete stop, mount in the usual way and move back into a canter without falling, confusing her or turning her in a circle.

'Stand up!' I called. Honey jerked her head back, but stood. I grabbed my stirrup with shaking hands and held it tight, pushing my left foot in, then bounced and sprang, gathering my reins in a second and asking Honey for a canter before I'd even found my other stirrup. The grey was ahead, but not by much. We made it to the finish line second. I dismounted again and threw my arms around Honey as the last four horses thundered across the line. We'd made it to the final round.

There was nothing I could do now but watch and wait. Who would I be riding against?

I walked Honey in circles, keeping her warm and limber, while the next two heats were fought and won. India and Rusty and a girl I didn't know on a dark pony came through in the third heat. A tall, thin girl with a dapple-grey mare and another Year Seven from my riding class, Sally, secured first and second place in heat four.

The final round was prepared with another two sets of stepping stones added to the first. The eight girls and their mounts were lined up. The starter explained that there would be six place ribbons awarded. Good, I thought: a six in eight chance of a ribbon. I strained my brain. What percentage was that?

Someone called my name.

I looked to my left, sharply. 'Get lost,' I hissed.

India smiled. 'Riding scholarship,' she mouthed, pointing to her own chest.

I fumed and did something I'd never done before. I took one of my hands off the reins and used it to let India know exactly what I thought of her. Then there was a noise and a rumble and, before I knew what was happening, the race had begun. Honey leaped in the air. I hadn't given her the signal to move, but everyone else was gone. I touched her sides with my lower legs and screamed, 'Go, Honey, go!'

I raised my hands higher up her neck, my eyes fixed on Rusty's chestnut rump at least two metres ahead of us. We were in last place.

We got to the stones just a second after the seventh rider. I didn't know who she was, but I knew I hated being last.

I kicked, wriggled and flipped and I was on the ground, running beside Honey.

I was on the first stone. I thought about jumping over a few but that was against the rules. I'd be disqualified for sure.

The girl with the dapple-grey tripped over one of her stones and had to go back. Sally had missed her stones altogether and was wheeling Mack in circles.

India was nearing her last stone and had a good chance for fourth place. I had no hope of anything but fifth. But Rusty was at least a hand taller than Honey. I realized that unless she was wearing springs in her boots there was no way India could vault. She'd have to bring Rusty to a complete stop. That's where I had a chance. I didn't care where I came now as long as I beat her.

That's it, I thought. I'll have to vault.

But I'd never done it on Honey. What if I messed it up?

India, on her last stone, took a second to twist around and look at me. That's when it happened. She fell from her last stone and knocked it over. I laughed aloud, despite myself. Now she'd have to go back to the beginning. I'd beat her for sure. She'd probably come last. And she deserved it.

But instead, she brought Rusty to a halt and began to mount. I couldn't believe it. India was a cheat! I jumped from my last stone. I had to vault. Honey was still trotting. I ran beside her and grabbed at my saddle. This was it. I sprang, from the very bottoms of my legs, and I prayed.

I made it about halfway up, then scrambled for my stirrup and pulled myself into the saddle. I'd done it! India was just jamming her foot into her stirrup. I drummed my heels against Honey's sides and screamed again. I knew it definitely wasn't correct riding technique, but I was desperate. I had to make it back over the finish line before India.

Honey stretched into a canter and I whooped with joy. I loved her and I loved this race.

We crossed the line a nose ahead of India and Rusty. I leaned forward and wrapped my arms around Honey's neck. She was breathing hard, we both were.

'Go line up for your ribbon,' a senior girl said.

I joined the line of riders and collected my fourth-place ribbon.

I looked over my shoulder. India was still at the finishing line and was arguing loudly with the senior girl there. I waved my ribbon in the air. She gave me the same hand signal I'd given her at the start of the race. Sometimes things have a way of ending as they began.

Emily raced from the stands to Honey and me and jumped up and down. 'Didja see that, Ash? She's been disqualified!' she cried.

I threw my right leg over my saddle and slipped to the ground, throwing my arms around her. Em hugged me back. It was unreal.

'Can I mind that for you?' Em said, holding her hand out for my ribbon.

'You bet,' I said. 'And you'll have plenty of your own one day.'

She looked up at me with moist eyes. 'D'you really think so?'

I grabbed her other hand. 'I know so.'

Honey nuzzled Em's shoulder and we both cracked up laughing.

'See,' I told her. 'Even Honey thinks you and horses were meant to be.'

Emily stroked Honey's nose. 'I reckon she could be right.'

The rest of the funkhana was the best time I'd had since arriving at Linley. Besides all those riding lessons and making two awesome friends and seeing the look on India's face after the Stepping Stones race. Honey and I competed in the individual Sack Race (where we had to race to a sack, hop inside and then lead our horses to the finish line) and came third in the final round, then came first overall in the team Ball and Bucket Race (where each rider collects a ball from one bucket and drops it in another bucket until the first bucket is empty and the second is full).

By the end of the day, Honey and I had added six new ribbons to our collection and Emily had been well and truly bitten by the horse bug. Not the kind of bug Claire was so afraid of, but the best kind, the being totally horse mad kind.

'Whenever you're ready for your first lesson, just say the word,' I told her as I led Honey to the wash bay. It was hot and she was sweaty and a hose-down was definitely in order.

Emily sighed. 'I will. Remember you said I've got six years.'

'But I didn't mean six years until you start. I meant six years to get as good as you can.'

I stood Honey on the concrete slab (no mud!) and turned on the hose. I sprayed her feet first — it was important to start there so she got used to the water temperature. After all, no one likes being thrown into a cold pool.

'Why would you come here, to Linley Heights and not ride?' I went on. 'I just can't understand it.'

'Try to understand this!' Emily's voice had changed. She sounded frightened.

'What?' I said.

'Emily Jane Phuong! *What* are you doing here?'

I peeked over Honey's back and saw a girl who looked just like Em (minus the glasses, with shorter hair plus a bit taller) bearing down on us.

'Mum told me to keep an eye on you. You promised her you wouldn't come near the horses and here you are.'

'Ash, this is my sister—'

'Mercedes,' I said.

Mercedes Phuong's eyes flicked to mine. She wore a look of total contempt on her face and her hands were on her hips. Her head kept doing this weird wobbling thing, just like I'd seen on TV. 'And *who* are *you*?'

'Mercedes, this is Ash, my friend—'

Murky shook her head as if she couldn't bear what she was hearing. 'I don't care who she is. Just some little Year Seven. You're all so annoying. Like cockroaches.'

I slapped my hand over my mouth. Becky's sister Rachael had been like this until she got back into horses, and then she became normal again. But Mercedes was clearly beyond horse-help hope.

'Get your sorry butt back up to the dorm,' Mercedes barked.

Em gave me a sad wave and fell into place behind her sister.

'I'm calling Mum and telling her everything and she is gonna totally spew,' Mercedes ranted. 'You're gonna be in for it now, squirt.'

I gritted my teeth. How dare she talk to Em like that? Em was my mate and mates stick up for each other. I looked at Mercedes and then at the hose in my hand. The running hose. The hose that was pumping dam water all over my horse. It only took a split second and a flick of my wrist and Mercedes Phuong was dripping wet.

'You idiot!' she shrieked. 'You rotten little—'

Then she said a few words I'd never heard anyone say out loud.

'Oops!' I said. 'I'm really sorry, I don't know what happened.'

Mercedes wiped at her face with her hands. Black streaky stuff ran down her cheeks.

'Is that mascara?' Emily said, pointing. 'Didn't you promise Mum you wouldn't wear make-up at school? I reckon if I called her and told her she'd be totally spewing. And you'd be in for it.'

'Ooh!' Mercedes stamped her foot, then marched off towards the school buildings.

'Wow,' I said, turning off the hose. 'She's, um, feisty.'

'You can say that again.' Em rolled her eyes.

'Hand me that sweat scraper, will you?'

'You were supposed to say it again.' Em giggled.

'Okay, hand me that sweat scraper, will you?' I pointed at the arced rubber scraper hooked on the wash bay rail.

Em laughed and passed it over and I began running it across Honey's body. Water ran down the scraper handle and onto the concrete.

'Wanna have a go?' I said.

'You bet!'

Em took the scraper and I showed her how to use it. 'It's like a squeegee. Just pretend you're washing a window.'

'A big, huge, hairy window.'

'That poos!' I moaned, as Honey made me a present on the once-gleaming concrete.

I cleaned up after Honey and grinned at Em. It had been some day. And I couldn't wait for the next one to begin.

twelve

Horse-People Power

'So when's this meeting?' Ricki hissed to me in Art class.

We were supposed to be reading up on ways of constructing clay pots. There was the coil method, where you stacked one snake-like piece of clay upon another and smoothed them together with your fingers; and there was the wheel, where you worked with a fat lump of clay, lots of water, your bare hands and hoped for the best. So far my best had resembled a crashed car. Ricki had sent her clay soaring across the room and onto the wall with a splat. So while everyone else was glazing their pots, chirping like chicks and listening to CDs, we were going back to the beginning.

'Tomorrow night,' I said, running my finger across the line of words on the page. None of them were making any sense. My head was choked with the meeting. It could be the beginning of the end of horses at Linley. 'I hope no one shows.'

'Wrong,' Ricki said. 'You hope plenty of horse supporters show.'

'Will you be coming? With your mum and dad?'

'My cousin's getting married this weekend,' Ricki said, pulling the lid off her pink highlighter. 'So I have to go to some party tomorrow night. My sister's a bridesmaid. The dress is SO disgusting! Whenever she puts it on at home I reach for my wand and try to magic some style into it.'

'Can't be that bad,' I said.

'You haven't seen it! You know what I wish?' Ricki rested her chin in her hand and sighed. 'I wish I could just *ooblakadoobla* and all this work would be done.'

'I wish I could *ooblakadoobla* Claire Carlson and her mother out of Linley Heights once and for all.'

I glared at my Art textbook. What use was it? It didn't tell me what to do about the meeting. I slapped it shut and put my head down on the desk with a thud.

Ricki patted my back. 'Don't worry. I'll take some pics on my phone of my sister in her horror dress. That'll cheer you up for sure.'

'No it won't. Nothing will.'

I banged my head gently on the desk, wishing that Becky were here. She'd come up with a brilliant idea in no time. I'd seen her stand up to the Creepketeers. She'd sort Claire out in ten seconds flat. Or Jenna. She'd always been good at thinking things up.

But Jenna was in the city. Becky was in Shady Creek. And I was here. It was up to me.

'I've got it,' I said. 'I've really got it.'

Ricki crinkled her nose. 'What've you got? A virus or something?'

'No.' I flicked the pages over in my workbook. 'I've got an idea.'

I stopped at a blank page and began to scribble. I was going to save the riding program. And I needed my friends to help me do it.

'How did you get all this stuff?' Emily stared at the sheets of card piled on my bed.

'Offered to clean the Art room for Mr Lowe.' I smiled triumphantly at her.

Em looked at me over her glasses. 'Pilfered all the stuff, more like.'

'Absolutely not!' Ricki declared. 'He was very generous. After a full dose of my incredible mind tricks we managed to convince him that he really didn't need those twenty sheets of brand-new card. Or the bottle of red paint.'

'Or the blue one,' I added.

Em crossed her arms. 'I've never met an Art teacher who gives away their supplies. It's like … a fish that can't swim or something.'

'Well, this one did,' I said. 'I suppose the fact that he agists a horse at the riding centre could have played a part.'

'No way,' Ricki said. 'It was my mind tricks. One swing of the crystal and he was ours!'

'Is he coming to the meeting tomorrow night?' Emily asked.

'Absolutely. He said that if he can't agist Rocky here, there's nowhere else. He lives in town, in a unit. He'd have to sell him or send him far away and hardly see him. At Linley he sees him every day.'

'I gave out all those leaflets, just like you said,' Emily said.

'Thanks, Em.' I grabbed her hand. I knew as well as she did that if Murk had caught her handing out my handwritten and hastily photocopied leaflets on coming to the meeting to save the riding program at Linley, she'd be in huge trouble. But her disguise of sunglasses and my riding helmet seemed to have done the trick.

'What do we do now?' Ricki said.

'We make these posters then hit the riding centre. We're gonna stick half up there and take the others to the meeting, to wave like those people on TV.' I was buzzing.

'Placards,' Em said.

'The people on TV are placards?'

'No, Ash, the protest posters are. Jeepers!' Emily rolled her eyes.

'Let's get to work! If I use my magic—'

'Ricki!' Em and I groaned at once.

Within an hour we had churned out twenty posters with slogans that ranged from *Save the Linley Riding Centre* to *Down with President Carlson* emblazoned across them in red and blue paint. (Ricki mixed her colours up to make purple, then decorated her posters with some of her magic glitter.) We dried the paint with Claire's hairdryer, stashed half the posters under my bed and ran to the riding centre with the rest.

Within moments of the posters going up, riders were gathering around muttering.

'They can't do this!'

'Nobody's gonna send my horse packing. This is his home.'

'If I can't ride here I'm leaving.'

'Well, make sure you show up at the meeting,' I shouted over the din. 'Mrs Freeman needs to hear what you think. And someone has to stick up for our horses!'

There were loud murmurs of agreement. A few of the riders shook our hands. We were going to win this. I could feel it.

Ricki had been picked up by her mum, and Em and I were in the dining hall. It was roast carvery night and my plate was piled high with roast lamb, potatoes, pumpkin, peas, carrots and gravy. Just like Nan would make.

'Do you think it'll work?' Em said.

I looked up from my plate. The dinner wasn't bad. Certainly an improvement on the baked beans, sausages and mashed potato we'd had the night before. 'It'd better. No riding program equals no riding scholarship equals no me.'

'And I'll never get a chance to ride.'

I slammed my knife and fork down hard. They bounced off my plate. 'We're not gonna let that happen, okay?'

Emily smiled. 'Okay.'

She took off her glasses and rubbed them on her T-shirt. 'They always fog up at dinner.'

'Hi, girls,' sang a voice.

'Hey, Claire,' I said, holding out my hand and wiggling my fingers. 'I've got lots of horse germs here. Want some?'

Claire took a step back, but wasn't fazed. Instead she was beaming. 'You were a busy bee in our room this afternoon.'

'Don't worry, I cleaned your hairdryer with a medicated wipe,' I said, spearing a pea on the end of my fork and dipping it into the gravy.

'I'm sure you didn't,' Claire said. 'But I was cleaning up—'

'As usual,' I muttered, popping the pea into my mouth.

'And while I was spraying under your bed—'

I almost choked on the pea. 'What did you do?'

Claire blinked, all innocence. 'I just cleaned away that mess you had under there.'

I stood up. 'Where are they?'

Claire shrugged. 'Where are what?'

'My posters, what else?'

'They were posters? I thought they were just rubbish. I took them to the recycling room. You're not mad, are you?'

Claire wasn't doing a very good job of hiding her delight. I looked from her to my plate and imagined dumping my entire dinner over her head. It was tempting. Very tempting. But I had a riding scholarship to keep and a hundred horses and riders to save.

'I'll get you,' I said.

'Miss Stephens! Ashleigh's threatening me!' Claire winked and ran over to the Year Seven house mistress. She put on a teary face and pointed in my direction.

'Don't worry, Ash,' Em said. 'I'll tell Miss Stephens what really happened.'

I was fuming. I pushed my plate away. 'Should've decorated her head with the veggies while I had the chance.'

'We'll find the posters,' Em said. 'And we'll all get behind you at the meeting.'

I shook my head. I knew we'd never find them. Claire had shoved all our hard work and our hopes into the nearest bin. I couldn't ask Mr Lowe for more supplies. It wasn't right. I couldn't let him down either. Hurt and angry as I was, I felt something stirring inside me. It was a plan. My best plan ever.

'We look like nutcases,' Emily groaned.

'We are nutcases. We're both certifiably horse crazy, yes?'

Em nodded miserably.

'Then walking into this meeting wearing our posters and saving the riding program should be no problem.'

I'd talked Emily into becoming a human placard. We'd torn neck holes in some old sheets of calico from the textiles room and used the last of Mr Lowe's donated paint on them. All we had to do was hold out our arms and the sheets opened. Emily was proudly (sort of) wearing *Save the Riding Centre* in bright red on her front and *If the Horses Go We Go!* on her back. I had *Down with President Carlson* on my front in blue and *Love Them* (I'd drawn a picture of a horse here) *or Leave Linley Heights* in a murky sort of purple on my back. I'd had no problem getting some of the riders to sign our sheets. Joe had been first in line. I wasn't only fighting for our right to ride. I was fighting for the riding staff's jobs as well.

'Six fifty-six,' Emily said, peeling back her sheet so she could see her watch. 'Meeting starts at seven.'

'You know, you're one of the only girls in school who still wears a watch. Everyone else has a mobile.'

'Ashleigh, I'm just about to publicly humiliate myself and all you can think about is whether I read the time from a watch or a mobile phone?'

'What's so humiliating about standing up for what you believe in?'

Emily sighed. 'Nothing.'

'Right! So let's go.'

'But Mum's here to pick me up for exeat.'

I shrugged. 'So's mine.'

'You don't care what people think, do you?'

'Yes, I do. But horses are my life. If Claire gets her way, I have no reason to be here. I would have no life here. I have to fight her. And I have to win.'

Emily stuck her hand out from under her sheet. 'Let's do it!'

We marched together towards the assembly hall where the meeting had been scheduled, singing at the tops of our lungs to the tune of the Linley school song:

Linley riders stand and fight
Ever riding, ever horse mad!

We burst through the doors of the hall. 'Save the riding centre!' I shouted, throwing my arms out to the sides so that everyone could read my slogans. Em did the same.

A large group of girls in riding gear stood on their chairs and clapped and whistled.

Another group, led by Claire Carlson, booed and waved placards. I squinted, trying to read what they said.

I slapped Em's arm. 'I can't believe it. What a little snake!'

'Ow!' Em rubbed her arm. 'What'd I do to deserve that?'

'Sorry, Em, it's just — ooh! Will you look at those posters!'

Claire and her mob were holding up our posters. But not the way we'd left them. They'd given them a makeover. They now read *Down with Linley Riding Centre* and *Save President Carlson*.

'Of all the low-down, dirty, double-crossing …' Em cursed.

'You sound like an old Western movie,' I said.
'That's it! She wants to play that way, I'll play.'

'Save the riding centre! Save the riding centre!' I chanted.

It wasn't too long before most of the audience, students and parents, had joined in. I caught sight of Mum in the crowd and rushed into her arms, squeezing her tight, so glad to see her I could have exploded.

'Look at you!' she said, a tear running down her face. She wiped it away. 'Are you thinner? Have you been eating?'

'Mum, you've got to help us. You've got to be on our side,' I said.

'Looks like most people here are on your side,' Mum said, holding my hands. 'Now shush, the principal's arrived.'

The hall settled and Mrs Freeman stood up to speak. She explained that she'd listened carefully to both sides of the argument. 'But while the majority of our students and parents do support the centre, there seems to be enough interest in closing the riding program to warrant further discussion.'

Claire clapped and embraced her mother.

There were gasps of disbelief from the riders, their instructors and their parents.

'Oh no,' I said. 'How can that be possible?'

Mum pressed her finger to her lips and wrapped her arm around my shoulders.

Mrs Freeman wished us a safe and enjoyable first exeat weekend and reminded our parents to sign us out.

I slumped in my chair, so disappointed. I'd truly hoped that we could crush the whole issue that night and it would never rear its ugly mug again.

'These things happen,' Mum said. 'Your principal has to try and be fair to everybody.'

'But this is the only school in Australia where I can—'

'Thanks for the posters, Ashleigh.' Claire glided past with her arm around her mother.

'Just go away,' I mumbled. 'Go spray yourself.'

'What was that about?' Mum said, frowning.

I sighed. 'It's a long story.'

'We've got the whole car ride home. Now where's this Emily you keep raving about in your emails?'

'She's right over here, she—'

I stopped dead.

Emily was where I'd left her, by the door. With her mum. She'd taken off her sheet and was staring at the floor. Her mum was shouting. Mercedes stood behind Mrs Phuong with her arms folded and an 'I told you so' look on her face.

'Maybe now's not such a great time to introduce you,' I said as Emily was dragged from the hall by her arm.

'Is she in some sort of trouble?' Mum looked concerned.

'We've got the whole car ride home, remember?'

Mum signed me out and stowed my overnight bag in the car boot. I was taking more homework with me than anything else. I'd said my goodbyes to Honey earlier that afternoon and made Joe promise to take extra special care of her.

'Her and a hundred others,' he'd said, winking.

I kept forgetting I wasn't the only horse-mad kid at Linley Heights.

'Home?' Mum said, once we were in the car.

I nodded. 'Creek Sweet Creek.'

As we drove away from the school, I could feel some of the stresses of the past few weeks ebb away. I focussed on seeing Becky and Pree, and spending as much time on the phone with Jenna as I wanted.

But I was so worried about Em. What was the hours-long car ride home going to be like for her? Would it be fun-filled, ringing with laughter? Or would it be one of those horrible silent journeys where everyone stares out of their window and can't wait until it's over?

Whatever happened to her, it was my fault. It was all my fault and I had to make it up to her. I would. That's what friends do, after all.

thirteen

Homecoming Scream

'You left Honey behind? What for?'

'I can't keep floating her back and forth,' I explained. Becky and I were playing with Toffee in my paddock, throwing him his chewed-up soccer ball and watching him catch it. 'It's a three-hour drive. She's just settled in the paddock too. Would you do it to Charlie?'

Becky frowned. 'No. But what are we supposed to do all weekend? I've got Pree sleeping over at my place. I thought we could all go riding.'

'Pree's sleeping over?'

Becky avoided my eyes. 'Sure.'

'Oh.'

I waited to be invited as well. We'd have a totally

awesome reunion, talk about old times and share some new fun together. After all, Becky and Pree might never have met if it hadn't been for me.

'I-I would've asked you too,' Becky stammered. 'But I forgot you were coming home this weekend, and I'd already asked Pree, and Mum said it's only one at a time.'

I didn't know what to say for a moment. I stared at the sky then down at the ground. There was a yucky tight feeling in my chest and throat.

'Maybe you could've emailed me about it,' I said sourly. 'We do get emails at Linley you know.'

Becky's face flushed. I could tell she was squirming and I was pleased with myself. The serious email drought from Becky had hurt me big time.

'I hardly ever get to use the computer, Ashleigh,' Becky said, folding her arms tightly across her chest. 'Rachael's a total hog. She's always on it chatting, or downloading music and stuff. Besides, you've only been away four weeks.'

I felt a wave of guilt wash over me. Rachael was a pain to live with — that was for sure. But I also knew that everyone at Shady Creek and Districts High School had their own email account. Hadn't she missed me enough to send me a quick email at lunchtime?

Toffee raced back with his ball and dropped it at my feet. 'Can I ride Cassata?' I said, hurling the ball. It was so flat now, it frisbeed across the paddock.

Becky shook her head. 'Since Rachael got that job at Shady Trails no one is allowed to touch Cassata. Not even me. Anyway, she finally met a horsy boy and they ride together all the time.'

'What about Bonnie?'

'Dad's horse? Are you serious? Mum reckons Dad loves Bonnie more than he loves her. He won't let anyone else ride her. Besides, she's too used to Dad now. I wouldn't want you to get hurt.'

I sighed. 'Maybe I could ride Toffee.'

Becky laughed. 'That'd be something.'

'I know!' I said, excited. 'Let's go over to Shady Trails and I'll ask Mrs Mac if I can take Calypso out.'

'But we've done the trails there a hundred times. I thought we could go horse swimming. I already told Pree and she's bringing her bathers.'

I collapsed on the grass. Toffee was finally bored with his ball and decided that chewing on my boot was a much better game. I shooed him away.

'I'll just stay here then,' I said. 'You guys go have a nice ride.'

'What are you gonna do?'

I shrugged. 'I dunno. Homework, I guess.'

'You get homework on the weekends?'

'Yup,' I said, brushing a fly from my nose. 'Don't you?'

Becky shook her head. 'Teachers have decided to go easy on Year Seven until we've settled in. We only get homework Mondays to Thursdays.'

I rolled over on my tummy. 'So what's it like, Shady Creek and Districts High?'

I was curious. I needed to know what to expect, just in case I wound up at school there. Until the whole riding centre issue was resolved, anything was possible.

'It's okay. We call it SCD High, just so you know. I'm not in any classes with the Creeps, thank goodness.' Becky picked at a long blade of grass and told me about the teachers and the subjects and the sports teams. She was playing netball and learning Mandarin.

'Don't you already know it?' I said.

Becky's face darkened. 'We know Cantonese. It's a totally different language. I can't believe you didn't know that.'

'Okay, okay,' I said. 'Sorry.'

A girl on a fat dun pony trotted down the driveway.

'Look, it's Pree!' Becky said, jumping to her feet. Her anger had melted. She jogged over to the fence and slipped through the rails. Priyanka Prasad wriggled out of her saddle, then slid down Jasmine's back and over her rump to the ground. My two friends hugged.

'Sleepover!' Pree shouted.

I joined them.

'Ash!' Pree shrieked. 'I can't believe it's you. Wow!'

She flew into my arms and we spun around while Becky hung back, watching.

'Have you heard this one?' Pree said. 'What goes black and white and black and white and black and white? A zebra in a revolving door! Do you get it?' She tipped her head back and laughed. I was dazzled once again by those brilliant white teeth.

'You cut your hair!' I said, touching her now shoulder-length black hair. I would have killed for that waist-long plait with the curly piggy-tail at the bottom. I didn't have to brush or wash or untangle it, though. And Pree had often complained about waking up in the morning with it wrapped around her face like a mummy's bandages.

'Out with the old, Ash, my friend.' Pree hooked her arm through mine. 'We going riding?'

'She left Honey at school,' Becky said.

Pree beamed. 'No problem. We'll just go to Shady Trails. Mrs Mac'll fix you up with a horse. Cally's your fave, right?'

'But I thought we were going horse swimming?' Becky said. 'We already organized it.'

Pree wrapped her arm around my shoulders. 'We can't go without Ashleigh. We'll do it next weekend.'

'I guess,' Becky grumbled.

'Don't worry about it,' I said. 'I've got tons to do here anyway. And Dad always complains that the only time the pool ever gets used is by the B and B guests, so I may as well swim here.'

'Better idea!' Pree said. 'We go to Shady Trails, get Ash a horse, ride until our butts beg for mercy, then come back here and swim together. Eh, Becky?'

'Whatever,' Becky said.

'Ash?'

'No worries, Preezy-Boo!' I said.

'I'll double you,' Pree said. 'Just let me dump my bag. And go get a helmet, Ash.'

I obeyed, but something wasn't right. In fact, there was a heavy feeling in my tummy like I'd eaten a tub of glue for breakfast. I'd only been away four weeks. I'd done that before, when I went to Waratah Grove. But I'd never been in any doubt that Becky was still my friend. Could things have changed that much in so little time? Part of me said 'no'. But there was another part, the part that was responsible for my instincts. And it was telling me that things just weren't polo in Shady Creek.

'Jase! You goobly-doobly, gorgeous-porgeous boy!' I poked at my baby brother's fat legs. He kicked them at me and grinned. 'Look at your toothy-woothy!'

'Ash,' Dad said, frowning, 'we don't talk baby talk to Jason, remember? We did all that reading before he was born and studies show that babies who are "gooblied" at are slower to speak than babies who are spoken to properly.'

'What did you speak to me?'

'We spoke "goobly".'

'I turned out all right.'

Dad gave me a look.

I was offended. 'What's that s'posed to mean?'

'Ash, it's been twelve years and you're still

speaking "goobly". With Jase, we have a chance to do things right!'

'Thanks a lot.' I slumped into my chair at the dinner table and watched Dad stirring. 'What's for eats?'

'Is that Linley talk?' Dad banged his wooden spoon on the side of the pot. Chunky red stuff fell back inside it.

'No, at Linley I'd walk in with my club, say "ooga booga" and eat a banana with the skin still on.' I rolled my eyes.

'You've grown since you started high school,' Dad said wryly. 'In cheekiness.'

I held up my palm. 'Talk to the hand!'

'That's it. You're going to Shady Creek and Districts High School next week with Becky!' Dad's face was as red as his cooking. 'There was none of this "talk to the hand" rubbish at Shady Creek Primary.'

I figured I'd be going hungry if I didn't tuck in my attitude, so I smiled my best smile and fluttered my eyelashes. 'I was just mucking around, Daddy.'

Dad tutted. 'Sure you were. I was expecting this teenage stage to kick in eventually. But you're not an official teenager yet so leave it at Linley.'

'Okay.' I plopped my head on my hand and picked at the tablecloth.

'Why are you here anyway?' Dad rummaged in the pantry. 'Surely we have rice. What kind of efficient household doesn't have rice?'

'I thought you knew more about that than me,' I began. 'But if you like, I'll give you the facts. When a mummy and a daddy—'

'Ashleigh Louise Miller!' Dad said, knocking his head on a shelf. 'That is not what I meant.'

I was surprised by his reaction. As a nurse he should have been cool about that sort of stuff.

'Why are you here, at home with me, when Becky and Pree are at Becky's house — that's what I wanted to know.'

'It's okay, Dad,' I said. 'They wanted me to come but I told 'em I really wanted to spend time here with you and Mum. And Jase, of course.'

Dad popped his head out of the pantry, like a meerkat. 'Really?'

I nodded. 'Really. I miss you guys a lot. Isn't it nice to be together again? As a family?'

'Well, sure, but the Ash I know would have been over at Becky's sleepover before you could say "pony".'

Dad gave me that look. The one where I know he's trying to read all my thoughts. I stared hard at the tablecloth. It was a really nice one now that I looked at it properly.

'We went to Shady Trails, I saw everyone, we had a ride, came back here for a swim and they left. It's cool, really.'

Dad raised one eyebrow. 'If you wanna talk …'

'I'll make sure I open with "goobly-doobly"!'

Dad reached across and tousled my hair. 'Cheeky!'

I ran my hands over my head, carefully returning every hair to its rightful place. 'I thought we agreed I was way beyond the tousling stage.'

'You agreed,' Dad said. 'As far as I'm concerned, I'll be tousling as long as I have life left in me! Thank heavens — rice! I thought we'd be mopping all this up with macaroni.'

'What is it?'

'Sweet chilli chicken.'

'Does that even go with macaroni?'

Dad grinned. 'No. I would have called it Roma Chicken if it had come to that!'

I ate my dinner, watched some colourful baby show on TV with Jason and gave him a bath while Mum hung out his stretchy baby suits on the line. Then I helped Dad with the dishes, agreed to get up early and do the breakfasts for the people in Room Two, had a shower, brushed my teeth and went to bed.

As I lay there, something was eating at me. It wasn't the sweet chilli or the fact that I hadn't done even one single scrap of the homework that was due on Monday morning. It was knowing that just a few streets away, at my best friend's house, there was a party going on and I wasn't invited.

Tears rolled slowly down my face onto my pillow. I let them fall. For the second time in my life I'd given up everything for horses. Jenna, Becky … What was I going to have to give up next? I tossed and turned, my chest aching and my head spinning. I could have lost Becky forever. Nothing had been said. It didn't need to be. Things had changed between us and I didn't know how to fix it. How could I even begin to fix it when I was hundreds of kilometres away?

I finally fell into a restless sleep. I dreamed of Becky, of holding her hands and feeling her pull away from me. I kept crying out to her, but the louder I called the softer my voice became, until finally there was no sound at all.

fourteen

Beginner's Luck

'Ready for your first practice session?'

Maryanne James beamed at me from the saddle. Her pure white horse, Cavalier, or Cav as she liked to call him, was ready for action and, like Honey, was decked out in protective exercise boots and coronet boots that fitted over his feet. Polocrosse was fast and furious and we wanted to spare our horses from injury, especially to any part of their legs. 'No hoof, no horse' my old riding teacher, Holly, had always said. She'd drummed it into my brain. I checked Honey's legs at least fifty times a day.

'Sure am,' I said. The truth was I was more than ready. This lesson wasn't just about learning the basics of polocrosse. It was my first real chance to push Becky to the back of my mind since exeat. 'Whaddya think?'

Maryanne examined Honey. 'Perfect, except for one thing.'

My heart plummeted. I'd wanted everything to be exactly right. 'What?'

'It's my fault. I should have told you.' Maryanne slipped to the ground and through the corral rails, then ran her hand down Honey's tail. 'It's this.'

I was offended. 'What's wrong with it?'

Maryanne laughed. 'Nothing, relax! We just need to tie it up. There's a special polocrosse tail-do. Check out Cav.'

'Gorgeous.'

'No, his tail!'

I left Honey with Maryanne and had a good look at Cav's tail. It had been plaited, folded in half and tied up in about five places with red wool. 'What's this for?'

'Keeps their tails safe. We wouldn't want a polocrosse stick getting tangled up in there.'

I winced. 'True.'

'Now we have to fix Honey's. She can't train or compete with a free tail. Know how to braid?'

'Are you kidding?' I grinned. Tail braiding was

one of my specialties. Just don't ask me to braid a human!

'Good,' Maryanne said. 'You get started on a nice neat braid, but go all the way down to the bottom of her dock. Then continue with a normal plait to the tip of her tail. I'm gonna go find a tail pull. Should be one in the tack room.'

'What's a tail pull?' I yelled after her, but she was gone.

I began braiding, taking strips of tail hair from the top of Honey's dock, braiding them together, then picking up a new strip on the other side. Before long I'd braided down to the bottom of her dock, just as Maryanne had said.

'Here.' A box of tiny clear braiding elastics was shoved under my nose.

'Just in time.'

I selected an elastic and wrapped it tight around the bottom of the braid, then shook out the rest of Honey's tail and separated it into three equal bunches. I plaited it to the very bottom and wrapped another elastic around the straggly chestnut tips. 'Now what?'

'Simple. You take the bottom of the tail, hook it inside the tail pull, yank it up through the braid and sew wool through it to hold it in place.'

'Huh?'

Maryanne grinned. 'I'll show you. But just this once.'

She held up what she called a 'tail pull' but really it was just an out-of-shape metal coat hanger. It looked like someone had grabbed it right in the middle of the long, flat bottom part and pulled down as hard as they could to make a teardrop shape with the hook on top.

Maryanne poked the end of Honey's tail through the bottom of the teardrop and pushed the hooked part underneath the braid at the top of her tail. She pulled the hook up and Honey's plait slid neatly up underneath the braid. All in the stamp of a hoof!

'Wow!' I was in awe.

Maryanne grinned. 'But wait, there's more!'

She pulled some long strands of fuzzy blue wool from her polo shirt pocket and handed them to me, then selected one from the top of the pile.

'Check this out.' She poked the wool through the tip of Honey's plait and through the top of her braid (which were now aligned), wrapped it around once and tied it ribbon-style. She did it again halfway down her tail, then again at the bottom.

'Another one for good measure.' She threaded a fourth strand in between the first and second strands. 'Should hold it. Usually I use one of those big wool needles, but it's in my kit. You'll be right.'

'Is wool strong enough? Shouldn't we use something tighter?'

Maryanne shook her head. 'Wool's plenty strong enough. Some players use that thick plastic tape, but that's so cruel. They do it up so tight the horse's circulation is cut off. How would you like to play soccer with tape wrapped so tightly around your legs they went numb?'

I bit my bottom lip, the way I always do when I'm nervous. I hadn't known, and I didn't want Maryanne to think I was stupid for asking. 'Sorry.'

'Don't be. I just get cranky when people don't treat their horses properly.'

I nodded. 'Me too.'

'You can use cable ties if you like. They're okay.'

I frowned. 'Cable whats?'

'Cable ties, that plastic stuff used to hold toys in boxes. One end gets poked through a little loop and pulled, and then you can't release it no matter what you do. Has to be cut with scissors, but it works well.'

She nudged my shoulder. 'Time to get going, Ash.' She slipped out through the rails and remounted Cav.

'Cav's real nice,' I said, leading Honey out of the corral. 'What is he?'

'A Camargue,' Maryanne said. 'Only one at Linley. Only one in the whole district, I'd say.'

'Camargue — the French horses?'

I sprang into the saddle and made myself comfortable, then walked Honey beside Cav to the outdoor arena. There was still enough time before the practice session began to give our horses a good warm-up.

'That's right. I'm impressed.'

I glanced quickly at Maryanne. 'By what?'

'Not many kids here know that. They all think he's an Andalusian.'

'I know a bit about the Camargue. They weren't recognized as a breed until 1968, but there are 15,000-year-old cave paintings of them in France.'

Maryanne stared at me. 'Wow.'

'I read a lot of horse books,' I said. 'And I seem to be able to keep all that horse stuff in my head. I just have a bit of trouble with all the other stuff, like all those dates in History.'

'You just gave me a date,' Maryanne said. 'So what's the difference?'

'But I love horses. I think about them every minute. I just don't have enough room for school stuff *and* horses.' I sighed, thinking about Mrs Wright and how she hated me even more since I'd barely scraped through my last assessment task in History. I mean, I liked History, but those dates!

'Why don't you try to bring the two together?' Maryanne said. 'Like if you're doing History, look for ways to research horses in the period you're studying. And if you're doing Maths, you could work out the probability of the Linley polocrosse team being state champs again this year. That sort of thing.'

I nodded, inspired. 'That's brilliant! I could study suitable terrain for horses in Geography or their impact on the ecosystem. There would be equine anatomy in Science, horses in Art, music to ride horses by, and how to make rugs in Design and Technology. It's a great idea.'

Maryanne laughed. 'I don't know how the School Board would feel about changing the entire curriculum to suit the horse mad. We're having enough trouble as it is with that Parents' Association woman.'

I grimaced and told Maryanne everything that had happened between Claire and me. The spray thing had been weird, the vacuum thing weirder, but the hatred now emanating from her side of the room was too much to bear. I was sending it back in equal doses, but neither of us was happy.

'So where are we at with the whole business?' Maryanne asked as she led the way into the outdoor arena.

I groaned. 'Mrs Freeman has given them the green light to put their concerns in writing. It'll be presented at the next Parents' Association meeting in a fortnight. If it passes it'll go on to the School Board. After that, I don't know.'

'Wow. That's serious mahooky.'

'You're not wrong.'

'Well, we can't do anything about it now except keep people aware and informed. Every rider is on our side. There's no way they can close the riding centre.' Maryanne sat quietly on Cav. 'Ready to warm up?'

I nodded. 'For sure.'

She smiled. 'Lead the way.'

I asked Honey to walk around the arena, and after finishing one lap we moved to a trot. We trotted three laps then changed rein through the diagonal — in other words, we changed direction by trotting diagonally across the arena in a 'Z' shape. Three more laps at a rising trot and we moved to the canter, working the arena in 'S' shapes or serpentines.

After ten minutes I asked Honey to return to the walk.

'Good warm-up,' Maryanne said. 'Let's hit the polocrosse field.'

There were four other riders ready to go by the time Maryanne and I arrived. Maryanne introduced me to Lily on Beau, Bridget on Max, Eden on Sapphire and Alysha on Love. They were all members of the senior team and Maryanne had asked them to let me tag along on their practice sessions. She thought it was a good idea for me to be thrown in at the deep end and that I'd learn more quickly from the older, more experienced players. I'd be training with my own team, of course. But right now Maryanne wanted me in up to my polocrosse stick.

'I think the best thing we can do for Ash is play a few chukkas for real,' she said. 'Keep it slower than usual, though. Your horse had polocrosse experience?'

I shook my head. 'Not that I know of.'

'I'll take that as a "no". We've got six so we have our two teams. We'll be red and blue. For red, if you could be Number One, Lil, Bridge do Number Two—'

'Beg your pardon?' Bridget said.

Maryanne blushed. 'I didn't mean it like that. And Eden, red Number Three, okay.'

'Righto, boss.' Eden saluted Maryanne, and the red team trotted away to their goal to discuss team strategy.

We were the blue team. Maryanne was Number One, I was Number Two and Alysha was Number Three. As soon as we grouped, Alysha's horse, Love, let out a high-pitched whinny and lunged at Honey. Honey snorted and kicked out. She'd never done that before. I closed my fingers in on my reins.

'No, Honey!' I scolded.

'Not her fault,' Alysha said, wheeling Love around. 'This one loves other mares. She wants to be best buddies, but she has the manners of a wild pig.'

Maryanne reminded me that Number Twos were only allowed in the midfield area.

Alysha grinned. 'No matter how many times you say that it's still hilarious.'

Maryanne rolled her eyes. 'Aren't we too old for toilet jokes, Al?'

'Never too old,' Alysha said. Then she laughed. 'Number Twos in the midfield area. Better watch out for those!'

I couldn't help myself, giggling into my glove despite Maryanne's sour face.

'Glad it's Love running around in all those Number Twos and not me!' Alysha was on a roll.

'Quit it,' Maryanne said. 'We've only got until seven, then they close the field.'

'Sorry, Mare.' Alysha bit her bottom lip. 'I'll be serious.'

'About time,' Maryanne snapped. 'We have to get moving before the horses cool down too much. I'm starting the game. Ash, your job is to chase and catch the ball, pass it to Al or me, and get it from the other team. Don't worry about any other rules for now, okay?'

I nodded. 'Okay.'

'Let's go.'

'Marrrrkkk!' Alysha cried.

Maryanne stared at her. 'What on earth are you doing?'

'I'm being the hooter.' Alysha gave me a wink.

Five riders (Maryanne was doubling as umpire) lined up. Maryanne threw the ball in and Alysha chased it immediately. Lily went for it as well, and there was a flurry of sticks then Lily had it in her racquet. Knowing she could only shoot for goal from the goal-scoring area, and that I wasn't allowed there, she cantered madly for our goal. I was stunned by the speed of it all. My mouth dropped open as Lily scored the first goal of the match in the first ten seconds of play.

'Wake up, Al, and defend the goal!' Maryanne shrieked.

'Aye, aye, cap'n!' Alysha called back, grinning.

The ball was returned to Maryanne and she threw it in again.

This time I was ready. I cantered into the mess of horses, my stick ready, my reins clutched in my left hand. I thanked the horse gods for all that Western training I'd had before coming to Linley — I'd got really good at neck-reining. I urged Honey towards the action but she shied away. I grabbed at my reins and lost my stick.

'You'll be needing this,' Eden said, handing me my stick. It had taken her only seconds to lean over, scoop it up and bring it to me. These were the hottest riders I'd ever seen.

Sapphire dived back into the fray and in seconds Eden had the ball. Al cantered after her, leaned across and hit Eden's stick hard upwards. The ball flew from Eden's possession and hit the ground, only to be picked up by Maryanne who turned Cav on his heels and cantered him for goal, shooting the second he set hoof in the goal-scoring area.

'Yes!' she cried. 'One all!'

She looked at her watch. 'Three minutes left of this chukka. Ash, I wanna see you doing something!'

Maryanne threw the ball in again, straight to me. I leaned across in the saddle holding out my stick, a bit like you'd hold out a frypan to catch a pancake. The ball fell into my net.

'Yay!' I cried.

'No time for "yays",' Maryanne yelled. 'Chuck it to Al!'

'Here, Ash, here!'

I could see Al about ten metres away. Sure I could never flick the ball that far (it was like pinging peas from a spoon — a really huge spoon!), I gathered my reins in my left hand and neck-reined Honey sharp right across the field, cantering for all I was worth.

'Now, now!' Al called.

I drew the racquet back in my right arm and let fly. The ball soared. Al stood up in her stirrups and scooped and it was hers.

'Yes!' I was so pumped. It was so exciting. And this was just a practice.

I cantered after Al, who was trying to break through the red team's defence and get to Maryanne. Bridget was closing in. I could see her getting closer to Al, her eyes on Al's stick where the ball, precious as a diamond, was nestled. It would take only one whack of Bridget's stick to dislodge it and the blue team would lose possession.

Al twisted around and, realising Bridget was on her tail, moved her stick around, a bit like she was stirring a huge pot of soup. This was to make it harder for Bridget to get a good shot at her stick. She only had to cover a few more metres and she could pass the ball to Maryanne.

Bridget closed in on Al's right and raised her stick. The horses were so close, but so focussed. It was like they were born for this game.

'Careful, Al!' I cried.

Al looked to her right and blew Bridget a kiss, then wheeled Love around to the left and cantered past Bridget, past me and then back down the field.

'Here!' Maryanne yelled.

Al raised her stick and — PING — the ball soared again, hitting the ground a few metres from Cav's feet. He leaped forward at once, shielding the ball with the left side of his body from Bridget. Maryanne scooped up the ball in less than a heartbeat and cantered for goal.

Eden was pacing across the goalposts on Sapphire. I knew from the rule book that they were two and a half metres apart. Things happened so fast in this game that Maryanne could score in the time it took Eden to blink. But it didn't look to me as though Eden was going to blink at all. Her eyes were fixed on the ball and on Cav's every step.

Maryanne slowed Cav to a more controlled canter and pushed him closer to the goalposts. Eden took the bait, racing over to defend her goal. Maryanne threw the ball over Eden's head to Al. Eden turned Sapphire on her heels. Al threw the ball back again and Maryanne flipped it forward for a goal.

'Oldest trick in the book, mate!' Maryanne cried.

Eden shook her head. 'I'll fix you up, James.'

'Take a break!' Maryanne called out, and gathered us in the centre.

'Typical,' Lily said, smiling. 'Call the game off when you're ahead.'

'Funny,' Maryanne said. 'Any questions, Ash?'

'Tons!'

'Fire away,' Al said, swatting a fly with her stick.

'Well, Cav's pretty short and Honey's fourteen two and Max looks like a giant. Isn't there a rule about size?'

Maryanne shook her head. 'Some teams are made up of families who ride all different-sized horses. But as teams are age-based, the ages of the players and the heights of the horses mostly match.'

'What about players?'

'Here at school, you're a junior and we're seniors. But out there in the real world you'd be on a junior team with players up to sixteen years old. As we're all seventeen, we'd be intermediates who are up to twenty-one,' Lily explained.

'The positions you play — do you have to stay the same all the time?' I asked. 'I mean, it'd be nice to have a go at goal-scoring one day.'

'You can play any position as long as the umpire

knows who's playing what,' Eden said. 'You can even change positions during a match as long as you do it between chukkas and the umpire and opposing team captain are informed. You have to change the number on your back as well.'

'Do horses ever crash?'

'Sometimes,' Bridget said. 'I came a doozy last year after a crash, remember, guys?'

Al whistled. 'We all thought you were a goner, Bridgey.'

'But there are lots of rules about who has right of way and about not crossing dangerously in front of another player and bumping.'

'Yeah,' Lily said. 'You're not allowed to bump or pull or push or anything that puts the horse at risk. You're allowed to push away only sometimes, in very particular circumstances.'

I sat in my saddle and rubbed my fingers in Honey's mane. There was a lot to remember. I was already having trouble with brain overload. How was I going to handle this as well? It was like eating a whole plate of broccoli at once. I could take a little nibble here and there, take my time, wash it down ... or I could stuff the whole lot into my mouth at once, nearly choke while I chewed it and require a polocrosse racquet to ram it down my throat.

Maryanne was watching me. 'What are you thinking?'

'Can we play some more?'

She looked to her team-mates. 'Whaddya reckon, guys?'

'I reckon we do some catching and throwing skills,' Eden said, examining her racquet at close range.

'Sounds like fun,' I said.

We stayed on the field, throwing and catching the ball at a halt, stand, trot and finally a canter, until Joe came and shooed us away at seven o'clock. By the end of the practice I was only missing half the balls, which wasn't too bad in my book.

We cooled down the horses and rugged them so they didn't get colds. Then, once they were cool enough, we let them drink and fed them in our private stalls, unrugged and groomed them, then re-rugged them and turned them out for the night, all the while weak with laughter from listening to Alysha's Number Two jokes.

It was unreal. But totally exhausting!

After a reheated dinner of spaghetti bolognaise,

I staggered up to bed and collapsed. Polocrosse was truly awesome. And this term I would play one real match. I looked at the calendar I'd pinned to the wall beside my bed.

Five weeks to go.

fifteen

Top of the Class

'Are you sure about this?'

I looked up at Emily who was sitting comfortably in the saddle on a bay school horse called George, and looking as if she'd been born there. It was a Saturday afternoon and good weather for riding. Not too hot, but warm enough to be nice out.

'Are you saying I shouldn't do this?' Emily asked.

I shook my head. 'Are you kidding? That's the last thing I'd say. I want you to do this. But I don't want you to get in any more trouble.'

I held George's lead rope tight and stroked his nose. He was twenty-five years old according to Joe, but he looked half that age. Joe put it down to a positive outlook on life, staying away from bad chaff and going to bed on time every night. He also mentioned enjoyable female company, but as George was a confirmed gelding I didn't know what female company could possibly have to do with it.

'The only thing that weekend of solitary confinement did was convince me I had to follow my heart.' Emily tugged at her stumpy ponytail and raised her chin. 'My heart is telling me to do this, Ash. You promised to teach me, so teach me.'

I shrugged. 'Okay, but if your mum grounds you for a whole weekend just for wearing a sheet, I don't wanna be around if she finds out about this.'

'Let her,' Em said. 'I don't care any more.'

'You can't say that about your mum. Even if she is scared of horses.'

I tugged on George's lead rope and he followed me out of the corral where I'd taught Em how to groom him and tack him up.

'I don't think it's being scared of horses any more. I think she reckons horses are a waste of time. I could be studying right now, see.'

'You could,' I said. 'Just as I could be trying to get a sound out of that violin that *doesn't* resemble a choking cockatoo! But isn't it great out here? You can just relax and think about nothing but the horse, and when he gets to know you and becomes your best friend it's like nothing can hurt you any more coz you know he loves you no matter what.'

'Thanks, Ash.'

I stopped George and turned around, looking up at Emily. 'For what?'

She shrugged and blinked a few times. 'You're the only one who's ever understood the way I feel about horses and learning to ride, and if I hadn't met you I know I wouldn't be here now.'

I was so amazed that for a minute I didn't know what to say. I just sort of patted her knee and said it was no problem. What I should have said was how brave I thought she was. She had everything against her — her whole family, her own fears. But she was still going after her dream and that was totally awesome. I'd never been through what she had. My parents had always backed me up in riding. Sure, they'd grumbled and complained and hated standing in the wind at gymkhanas and couldn't tell a fetlock from a forelock, but I was here at Linley Heights to ride and they'd been nothing but stoked for me.

My heart ached for Emily. After all, the person you are is the only one you know how to be. It doesn't matter if someone else thinks you should be different. All that comes of trying to change someone is misery, and Em did look miserable a lot of the time.

But not right then. From the first moment I'd introduced her to George, through to showing her how to lift his foot or teaching her how to test the fit of his bridle (three fingers between the horse's cheek and the throatlash is best), she'd done nothing but beam. And now that she was actually in the saddle for the first time in her life, it was like she'd swallowed the sun and it was shining out through her teeth!

'Feel good?' I asked.

'You've got no idea,' Em said, giggling.

'I might have some clue.'

I led her into the round yard. I had her first lesson all planned out. I was going to teach her to mount and dismount correctly, then try and get the best possible seat out of her. Then lead her around a few times, making sure she felt comfortable and confident. Finally I was going to try lunging George at a walk and let Em have a taste of riding for real.

George stood quietly while I let the lead rope slip through my fingers until I was holding on to the very end of it, then I closed the gate behind us. He was well used to beginners and very calm, but as a rider and a teacher I had to be on my guard. Em's safety was entirely my responsibility. I didn't want to put her at risk. An open gate plus a frightened horse could easily equal disaster — the last thing I wanted for my friend. Especially as Mercedes Phuong (aka The Global News Service) didn't need to hear about Emily falling and having to go to the school nurse, or even breaking a bone … I stopped myself. Was this what worrying about your own kids was like? I didn't know. But I didn't like it.

'You look great up there,' I said once the gate was closed. 'But you're going to have to come down.'

Emily's face fell. 'Is it finished already?'

I laughed. 'We're just starting. As in from the very beginning — mounting and dismounting.'

Em brightened at once.

'Some riders take only the right foot out of the stirrup when they dismount but you're going to take both out.'

'What do you do?'

'Both,' I said. 'Always have. You'll learn a few ways and eventually settle on one that you're really comfortable with. So what you're gonna do is lean forward, sort of balance your weight on your right hand — no, don't let go of the reins. Now, swing your right leg over his rump — that's it! Now let yourself drop, still holding the reins, the pommel too if you need to, and bend your knees slightly when you touch the ground.'

Emily did as she was told and executed an impressive first dismount.

'How was that? Did I do it okay?'

I'd never seen her so excited.

'You did great,' I said. 'Better than great!'

Em clapped herself, then hugged George's neck. George looked pleased with the attention he was getting.

'Now you're gonna have a crack at mounting.'

'Didn't I already do that?'

'No, I gave you a leg-up. That's not the same as getting into the saddle yourself.'

Em looked up at George's back. 'How high is this horse again?'

'He's about thirteen hands high, I'd say. Pretty good size for you.'

'How do I get my leg over from here on the ground? I'm not made of rubber, you know.' Em gave me a look.

'I'll get you a mounting block. Some riders can spring into the saddle from the ground. Others use mounting blocks. It doesn't matter as long as you get in the saddle safely and comfortably for you and the horse.'

'Everyone'll laugh at me if I use that,' Emily said, pointing at the mounting block I was dragging over. It was like a huge round black plastic bin with two steps built in and a handle. 'It looks like it's for babies.'

'Rubbish,' I said. 'I know plenty of riders, including grown-ups, who use them. It's a whole lot better to mount with this and not pull on the saddle or thump down onto the horse's back, than to try from the ground and hurt your horse.'

Em nodded. 'True.'

I positioned the mounting block beside George so that the tallest step was just under the stirrup on his nearside.

Em sized it up. 'So, what do I do?'

'First we have to make sure the horse is standing square.' I stepped back and examined George. 'Some horses take a step forward when the rider mounts and the rider thinks they're being bad, but they're only trying to balance themselves. If George is resting a leg or has one foot too far back or forward, your weight could make him take that step.'

George's offside foreleg was too far back. I tugged gently on the reins and he took a small step forward. Now he was square — all four legs were evenly placed on the ground, making a square shape.

'Up you go,' I said, patting the top step.

Emily stepped up onto the top of the mounting block. 'Now what?'

'Take the reins in your left hand and push your left foot into the stirrup.' I held the stirrup for her. 'Nice boots.'

She smiled. 'Thanks for the loan.'

'No worries! Now, stretch your right hand as far over the saddle as you can. Some people grab hold of the pommel, the front part of the saddle, here.' I patted the pommel of George's saddle. It was an old all-purpose leather saddle so the pommel wasn't as high as some other saddles, like endurance or stock saddles, but it was enough to hold onto in an emergency! 'But that can pull at the horse or shift the saddle. It's better to try to mount without doing that.'

'No pommel. Got it.'

'Now put your weight onto your left foot, lift your leg over, like you're getting on a bike, and sit as gently as you can. You did it!'

Emily looked so proud. I knew I'd never forget her smile.

'Sitting here, it's like … like …'

'Coming home?'

Em nodded. 'Yeah, that's it — coming home.'

'Find your right stirrup.'

'Find?'

'Put your foot in the stirrup. One day I'll be lunging you in here at a canter and you won't be allowed to have stirrups at all. But not today.' I held the right stirrup still for Em while she wriggled her foot inside. 'Perfect — you look great.'

I ordered George to stand still (not that I needed to worry — he was nearly asleep) and walked around horse and rider, checking out Em's seat — the way she was sitting in the saddle. For a first-timer she looked pretty good, but I had a few pointers for her. I knew she might forget much of what I told her — after all, the bliss of being in the saddle for the first time tends to wipe away any memory of the actual lesson. But Em was smart. I was hopeful she'd store it in there somewhere.

'We're gonna talk about your seat,' I said. 'That doesn't just mean the way you sit. It's your whole body position, even the way you hold your head.'

'Whoa,' Em said. 'Sounds hard.'

'It's not hard, but it is the most important thing you'll ever learn about riding. A good seat will help you get the best out of your horse, whether you're pleasure-riding or competing.'

'Tell me what to do.' Em looked determined.

'You're sitting in the deepest part of the saddle, the centre, which is great, but you need to sit up straight. You're slouching a bit. You have to imagine that someone's drawn an imaginary line from your ear down to your hip and then to your heel.' I tapped gently on Em's hip and heel as I spoke.

'Lines. I can do that. I'm okay in Maths.' Em looked more confident now.

'Just okay? Aren't you some kind of child prodigy in Maths?'

Em frowned. 'Who told you that?'

'Word gets around,' I said, grinning.

'Knees,' I said next, moulding Em's legs like a doll's. 'They should be in firm contact with the saddle, lower leg maintaining a light pressure with the horse's sides. Your stirrups could come up a notch — they should be neither too long nor too short for working on the flat — balls of the feet on the stirrup iron, heels pointed down ... good! Now don't move a muscle!'

'Really?' Em said.

'Nuh, that'd be impossible. But always try to remind yourself to correct your seat. Now for the arms!'

Emily moaned. 'I'm getting sore.'

I grinned wickedly. 'Wait 'til tomorrow. I couldn't walk for three days straight after my first riding lesson.'

'How old were you?'

'Six.' I smiled, remembering Pepper, my first-ever school horse. He was an old blue roan pony gelding, as patient and kind as a grandpa. Everything I was teaching Em now I had learnt on Pep.

'Shoulders square, upper arms against your body, hands steady but not stiff. Nice. Now we'll fix those reins!'

I twisted and bent Em's hands into the perfect position, feeding the reins between the correct fingers, making sure her little fingers were opposite each other and her wrists were supple.

'Pony ride time,' I said. I checked that the lead rope was securely clipped to George's bit and clicked my tongue. 'Get up, old man.'

The horse took a step forward.

'Ooh! This is so cool!' Em said.

'It's gonna get cooler,' I said, leading her on her first lap of the round yard.

Three laps later Em was ready for something new.

'Ready to walk?' I asked.

'What do I have to do?'

'Today, nothing. I just want you to get a feel for the horse. I'll be driving, okay?'

I unhooked a lunging cavesson from the wall of the round yard and fitted it over George's bridle. The cavesson looked just like a halter with the exception of the metal ring in the centre of the noseband. I clipped a long lunge line to the ring and held it up to show Em, then unclipped the lead rope from his bit and tossed it to the fence of the yard.

'I'm going to lunge you, just at a walk. Lunging is when we work the horse in a circle in both directions. This line helps me to control George.'

I picked up a long lunging whip from the sandy floor of the round yard. There was usually one left lying around for anyone to use.

'You're not going to hit him, are you?'

I shook my head. 'No way. I hold the line in my left hand and the whip in my right and just follow him with it. Keeps him awake. Ready?'

Em nodded stiffly, terrified to mess up her seat. 'Definitely. I've been waiting practically my whole life for this, Ash.'

I raised the whip just off the ground. 'Walk on!' I called.

George took a step forward, then another. Emily giggled. 'This is so great!'

'Try to move with the horse. You'll only fall off if you're stiff. That's better. Hey, you're really good. You're a natural!'

I lunged George a few times clockwise, then anti-clockwise, then asked him to stop. 'Whoa!'

George stopped at once. He was such a good boy. I gathered up the lunge line and approached his head, rubbing under his forelock. 'Well done to you.' Then I looked up at Em. 'And to you too.'

'That was so incredible,' Em squealed. 'Just so totally, utterly wonderful! When can I have another lesson?'

'Whenever you want. Tomorrow or the next day. I'm here all the time, remember? Time to dismount. Let's see if you remember how to do it.'

Em dismounted exactly the way I'd shown her.

'I'm telling you, you're a natural. You'll whip my butt by the end of the year.'

I raised the saddle flap and loosened George's

girth — a reward for his hard work. He'd have a nice groom and a feed as well, but that would be after he'd cooled down and been lightly rugged.

'You lead him home,' I said. 'To the corral. That's where we untack him and turn out his saddlecloth to dry and air. Then we take him to his own stall.'

Em listened carefully to my instructions on leading — to hold him by the reins under the chin with her right hand, the left hand picking up the slack and never twisting it around her fingers. To tell him to walk on. To stand close to his near shoulder and make sure she walked beside his shoulder. Then she did it. I was so proud of her and so happy for her. And to think we'd pulled off an entire lesson without a look-in from Murky or India. It was too good to be true.

Emily's lesson continued long after she'd dismounted. In that one afternoon she learned to untack, rub down, rug, cool out, measure feed and turn out. A very successful, but totally tiring beginning to her dazzling horsy career.

'When you're representing Australia at the next Olympics, make sure you say "hi" to me from the podium when you get the gold medal. Even a wave would do.'

Em shook her head. 'I'll never be that good. Even though I want to. You know as well as I do, I'll be a doctor or a lawyer in some big city.'

I stopped and grabbed her shoulders. 'Enough! You want this so much. You have to go for it!'

Em closed her eyes and sighed. 'You don't understand, Ash. They've worked it all out, even down to what I'll specialize in. I sure don't remember gold-medal horse riding being very high on their list.'

'I don't get you,' I said. 'Why do you let them decide what's going to happen with your life? I never would.'

Em's eyes flashed, then turned so cold I was afraid she'd crack her glasses. 'If you're really my friend you'll let up. I get heaps from them. I don't need it from you too.'

Em stalked away, back up towards the school. I stood there watching her go. How could she get so mad at me but not tell the people who were making her miserable what she felt? It didn't make any sense.

Then again, wasn't I, Ashleigh Miller, who'd sworn she would never let anyone make her feel miserable (or sworn to try at the very least), letting the same thing happen? I shuddered from the top of my head to the tips of my riding boots.

Becky.

I decided then and there. I was going to find out what was wrong with Becky. That way I could fix everything. It was so simple it was ridiculous. All I had to do was press one button on my mobile phone, take a deep breath and ask her. Easy.

sixteen

Campaign Trail

'Heard the latest?' Claire said smugly.

I gave her the most withering look I had in my repertoire. It was hard to look tough when I was wearing my *I ❤ Horses* pyjamas, but I did my best. 'The latest what?'

'The latest on the campaign.'

I feigned ignorance. 'What campaign?'

'Don't pretend you don't know what I'm talking about. The campaign to close the riding centre.'

I yawned, huge as a hippo. 'Oh, that. I thought that was all dead and buried.'

Claire's face went pale. 'Don't say those words in front of me. It's bad luck!'

I closed the novel I was reading for English and shrugged. 'Which words — *I thought?*'

'No!'

'*Was all?*'

Claire shook her head. 'No, no!'

I smiled, even though I knew I shouldn't. 'Do you mean *dead and buried?*'

She put her hands over her ears. 'Don't!'

I started to sing. 'Dead and buried, dead and buried, deaaaaad and buried!'

'You're wicked!' she shrieked. 'I'm telling my mother about you. How you say nasty words and tease me and wear those repulsive boots in my room!'

I rolled my eyes and slapped my novel down on the bed. I'd always been kind of messy at home (okay, okay — a lot messy), but here at boarding school, without Mum to chuck fits over the 'uninhabitable condition' of my bedroom, I'd let things go. Miss Stephens, our house mistress, had given me a little talking-to, but it hadn't made any difference. I'd been at Linley Heights for six weeks and already my desk was covered in junk and I was forced to do my homework on my bed.

'It's my room too, you know,' I said.

I lay flat on my bed and stared at the ceiling, wishing I was sharing a room with Em (we'd made up after our 'disagreement' and had already scheduled her next riding lesson). There were thirty-four school weeks remaining. I didn't think I could make it to the end without inflicting some kind of serious bodily harm on my crazy roommate.

'Well, I wish it wasn't. And once I tell Mum about this, you'll wish it wasn't too.'

I rolled over and stared at the wall, turning my back on her. 'Already do.'

'I won't have to put up with you too much longer anyway,' she gloated.

'Best news I've heard all day.'

'Don't you wanna know why I won't have to put up with you?'

'No.'

Claire sniffed. 'I'm gonna tell you anyway. My mum — you know she's the president of the Parents' Association — she had a meeting with Mr Sinclair today, the chairman of the School Board.'

'So?' I scratched at a blob of hard, dried paint on the wall. I was trying to make Claire think I didn't care. But I was terrified. My heart was thumping so loudly I was having trouble hearing her.

'So his daughter's an Old Girl as well, and when she was in Year Nine she fell off one of those wretched school horses and broke her collarbone.'

'She should have been more careful then,' I spat.

'Don't you see?' Claire continued. Every word she said was like a needle poking into my heart. 'He hates horses now. He wanted to close the riding centre back then, but he was only a parent. Now that he's the chairman of the Board he can do whatever he wants.'

'I'll send him an SMS congratulating him.'

The blob of paint was gone now, but so was my fingernail. I'd scratched so hard I'd managed to rip it away. It was bleeding a bit and stinging. But I wasn't going to let Claire see I was hurting.

'You do that. While you can. Once those disgusting animals have gone from here, you'll be gone too. You can all stink somewhere else.'

I sat up. 'I don't stink!'

'Smelled yourself lately?' Claire said, and pulled her vacuum cleaner from under her bed. It was her night-time ritual to vacuum her side of the room before she went to sleep.

I got into my bed and pulled the sheets up to my ears, trying to block out the sound.

'Your turn to switch off the light,' Claire said when she'd finished.

'If you want the light off, you do it,' I grouched.

I closed my eyes and tried to pretend she wasn't there, that I was back home in my own room, with Jase in the room next door and Mum and Dad down the hall. Honey was in her paddock under my window, and if I concentrated really hard I could hear her tearing at the grass. Toffee was rubbing up against the fence, trying to Houdini himself out of his night rug, and there was a kangaroo family grazing on the front lawn.

I must have fallen asleep soon after that. I dreamed. Of running to the riding centre, panic ripping at my lungs, and finding it empty. No horses, no Joe, no Demi, no riders ... nothing. I ran from stall to stall, paddock to paddock. I couldn't find Honey. I screamed her name but all I could hear was the echo of my own voice. It was like the world I knew had died and there was nobody left to grieve for it but me.

'Sleep well?' Demi James asked me.

I glowered at her from under my helmet. It was time for my group riding lesson and I was still a B. 'Are you kidding?'

She gave me a look. 'What happened?'

'It's a long story.'

'Well, leave it at the gate. We don't bring our problems into the arena, or anywhere else around horses for that matter. The horse doesn't need you lumping your issues on her.'

I glared at Demi and grabbed a handful of Honey's mane. Honey was my soul mate. She always listened to my problems and had never complained about it once. But I knew Demi was right.

Demi turned to address the class. 'Today we have a great lesson. We've done our warm-up and now we're going to be working on our transitions. Who can tell me what a transition is?'

India's hand shot up. 'When you change pace.'

'Good. Now who can give me an example of a transition?'

I knew the answer. I'd known the last one. But I was too tired and drained to hold up my hand.

'India again?' Demi smiled at the biggest pain in Year Seven. Well, one of the biggest.

'Halt to walk, walk to trot, trot to canter—'

'We get it,' I muttered.

'Ashleigh!' Demi snapped. 'If I want your contribution I'll ask for it.'

India grinned. I was crushed. I hadn't meant to say it so loudly. And Demi was the last person in the universe I wanted to dislike me.

'I'm sorry, I—'

'You'll be especially sorry tonight,' she cut in. 'Two pages of research notes to be handed to me first thing tomorrow on one female Australian equestrian. Enjoy.'

I blushed, making up my mind to turn in the most dazzling two pages of research notes Demi had ever seen. And to shut my mouth.

'Transitions,' Demi said. She sounded flustered and it was all my fault. 'A perfect transition should be achieved with practically invisible signals from the rider to the horse. Many of you kick and pull and whip and dig with spurs. But I can't remember the last time I saw a champion dressage or Western rider flailing about on their horse in order to get them to speed up or slow down.'

'I was taught to pull on the reins,' whined Natalia.

'You were taught wrong. And now you're going to do it right.'

Demi was mounted on her dun gelding (I'd asked her his name — Cougar). She instructed us to all gather in the middle of the arena and walked him around us for half a lap, then halted in the right-hand corner, near the mirrors.

'Did anyone see me pull on the reins?' she asked.

'No,' we chorused.

'Transitions should appear smooth and effortless. I am giving him signals, you know I am, and you can see the result of those signals when he increases or decreases his pace or halts. But when you're competing, those signals should never be visible. They should be as subtle as possible.'

Cougar walked on, then trotted, then cantered around us. He halted, reversed ten paces, moved straight into a canter, then executed a perfect flying change without me detecting a single movement from Demi's legs or hands. I'd been riding for six years, half my life, and I had never ridden like that. Right at that moment, I didn't believe I ever would.

'Anyone see anything that time?' Demi asked.

'No.'

'Now it's your turn. I want you in single file, anti-clockwise around the arena to begin with. India, you lead out.'

India turned and stuck her tongue out at me, shaking her head so it wobbled. Her tongue was pretty long and probably useful for catching the flies and mosquitoes and every other disgusting thing toads eat. I smiled warmly at her and waved.

'Make good use of the mirrors,' Demi went on. 'They are not there to serve as lip-gloss checkers — by the way, any of you decide to wear make-up of any kind to class again and you'll be mucking out the corral at the end of the day.'

I sniggered. India was wearing an entire pot of gloss on her lips.

'The mirrors are there for you to see exactly what you look like in the saddle. Keep at least three horse lengths between each of you. This isn't a nose-to-tail trail ride. Good. Now halt.'

I squeezed my legs against Honey's sides but didn't give with my hands. She stopped.

'Good halt, Ashleigh. Natalia, stop pulling on her mouth. Look at the way she's resisting you.'

I twisted around. Natalia's horse, Rosie, was still walking forward, her head held high.

'The more you pull at her, the more she'll fight you. Do you see the way she's thrown up her head and neck? That's called "hollowing against the rider". Always ask with your legs first, then go to the hands as a last resort.'

Rosie stopped at the tail of the horse in front of her.

'See — she stopped,' Natalia said.

'Only because she was about to go up Corey's butt,' I said. 'That had nothing to do with — sorry!'

Demi glared at me. 'Four pages!'

A ripple of chatter went through the class. I was the first person to ever be punished by Demi. Nobody wanted to be me.

'I need a volunteer. Ashleigh!' Demi waved me forward.

I wanted to make the best halt-to-walk transition I possibly could. I was already up to my eyeballs in trouble with Demi and I had the feeling she'd volunteered me so she could crush me in front of the class. I didn't want to give her one single opportunity to do so. I squeezed both legs against Honey's sides and gave with my hands at the same time, letting them move forward. Honey walked towards Demi.

'I hope your halt is immaculate!' Demi said. 'After all, you seem to be full of free advice for everyone else today.'

I gritted my teeth and tried to block out the sound of India's laughter. So far in the lesson, India had waggled her tongue at me and laughed and Demi hadn't seemed to notice. Was it the Old Girl versus New Girl thing again?

Demi was watching me like a hawk. 'Halt!' she said.

I squeezed again, again not giving with my hands and Honey halted.

'Lucky for you,' Demi said. I couldn't help feeling she was disappointed I'd managed a perfect halt. She addressed the class. 'Ashleigh's going to demonstrate the transitions for all of you. Pay close attention. Look up, Ashleigh! Many riders make the mistake of staring at their horse's head. It'll still be in the same place you left it after your ride.'

I blushed for the second time that lesson, but tried to concentrate on my seat. Every word I'd said to Em during her first ride marched through my head. I hoped I was sitting as well as I'd expected her to.

'Walk on!' Demi said. 'You should be squeezing your legs against her sides, asking for the transition. The hands move forward with the forward movement of her head and neck. Good. Now that she's moving, relax your legs but keep those hands moving backwards and forwards with her. Don't pull on the reins!'

'I wasn't!'

'Six pages.'

I stared at Demi, open-mouthed. This was unbelievable. I felt hot salty tears springing up and squeezed my eyes shut tight in an effort to kill them. One determined tear ran down my cheek. I shook my head, trying to shake it away. The last thing I wanted was for India McCray to see me crying.

'Keep your head still!' Demi said. 'The horse is guided by your head — she'll go in the direction you look.'

I gave Demi a look that I hoped she'd choke on. I'd been saving it for India but couldn't hold it any longer. Demi either didn't notice or ignored me.

'Good. Ask for the trot.'

I repeated the movements. Honey responded immediately. I made a mental note to give her an entire bag of carrots and a massage at the end of the lesson.

'Canter right circle. Her off leg will be leading so you'll use your inside rein to ask her to flex right and your outside rein to control the pace. Your outside leg is behind the girth, your inside leg is on the girth. Use your seat bones!'

Honey cantered in circles to the right, then, when Demi barked at us again, I changed direction on the diagonal and cantered left. It was some of the best riding I'd ever done and, no matter what her assessment, I was proud.

'Next transition — ask for the trot.'

I squeezed with my lower legs again, this time reducing the amount of give in my hands — I didn't allow them to follow Honey's head and neck movement as much. This wasn't pulling, but restraining. She trotted. I wanted to jump off right there and kiss her!

'Walk!'

I repeated the action. Honey walked.

'Halt.'

Honey responded again to the signals. She was the best horse in the arena, in the school … in the entire world! She knew I was in trouble and she was there for me, plucking me out of it. My Honey horse. My hero.

I was in front of Demi now. Although I wanted to stare at the arena floor, anything to avoid her eyes, I looked up and ahead. Demi moved Cougar right beside Honey and leaned towards me. I sat still, not moving. If she expected me to be afraid, or to flinch or run away, she was wrong. Very wrong.

'That was incredible riding, Ashleigh,' she whispered. 'Be the best you can be. Don't be drawn into silliness by the others. You're only putting yourself at risk. You can't afford to do that.'

I looked at her then, right into her eyes, and I understood. I was a scholarship student. I had to justify my presence at Linley Heights School. I couldn't mess this up.

'It'll never happen again,' I said quietly. 'I'll hand in the six pages in the morning. Is there anyone in particular you'd like me to research?'

Demi raised her eyebrows. 'Mary Hanna?'

'Done,' I said. It'd be an honour to research one of Australia's foremost dressage riders. 'And thank you.'

Demi smiled. 'You're welcome.'

She sent me back to the group and continued the lesson. India's gleeful looks and Natalia's hateful ones didn't bother me at all. I knew why I'd come to Linley and I knew what I had to do. I was here to ride and I would ride well. No matter what.

seventeen

Mysterious Ways

'What happened to you yesterday?' Ricki Davis asked, winking out at me from under her mess of long dark curls. I would have killed for her hair. 'I didn't see you all afternoon.'

We were sitting in the Year Seven section of the playground eating our lunch. I bit into my cheese and tomato sandwich.

'Long story. Starts with India. Ends with a six-page punishment. Fill in the blanks.' I eyed off Ricki's lunch. 'That looks totally delicious.'

'Do you want it? Have it — truly, it's okay.'

Ricki offered me her lunch box. It held a bright red and green salad, meatballs, a slice of flat round bread and a creamy dip. It smelled wonderful.

I wrinkled my nose. 'Don't tempt me.'

Ricki shoved it closer. 'Take it. I had this for dinner last night. Tell you what. Trade me half of your lunch for half of mine.'

'Deal.' I handed her half of my sandwich.

Ricki held it to her nose. 'I've always wanted to know what boarders' food tastes like.'

'Well, I can't remember what real food tastes like, so we're a good match,' I said, accepting the lid of Ricki's lunch box, which she'd heaped with salad — tabouli, she called it — meatballs, some of the hommus dip and half of the bread.

'Scoop up the tabouli with some bread,' she told me. 'And the meatballs taste amazing when you dip them in the hommus.' Then she took a bite of cheese and tomato sandwich, chewed carefully and swallowed. 'Well, I always wondered, and now I know.'

I stuffed some tabouli in my mouth. It was crunchy and tangy and delicious. I'd never tasted anything like it. 'This is so good.'

Ricki grinned. 'Come to my place for dinner any time. My mum loves feeding people. It's like her hobby or something. She even goes to cooking classes for *fun*! Actually, that's where she learned to make the tabouli. So, where's Emily?'

'Maths extension, where all the geniuses go. She has a lesson two lunchtimes a week.' I ate some more. 'Wow, this is so tasty. We had *fish fingers* for dinner last night!'

We finished our lunch and Ricki showed me her latest trick. It was a magic colouring book. One tap of her wand and the magic word (which for Ricki could be anything from *abracadabra* to *oongalaboongala*) and the pictures appeared or disappeared.

'That's so cool!' I said, giggling. 'You're really good. You could be a professional.'

'I will be,' Ricki said, packing her trick into her bag. 'A professional—'

'Idiot!' interrupted a familiar voice. India McCray.

'Can't you just leave us alone?' I said, rolling my eyes. I stood up and dusted off my backside.

Ricki followed suit, then took out her magic wand and waved it over India's head. 'Maybe if I say the magic word, she'll turn into a person! *Hullabaloola, bobbitty boo*! Nuh. Still a jerk.'

India rolled her eyes and nudged Chelsea. 'Whaddya reckon, Chels? Can we leave these two weirdos alone?'

'Made for each other!' Chelsea said.

I snatched at the handles of my schoolbag.

'C'mon, Ricki. Let's get out of here before it happens to us.'

India grabbed my arm. 'Before what happens?'

I shook her off. 'Before we turn into morons like you.'

'Oooh,' India sang, 'thinks she's good. Thinks she's clever.'

'Whatever.' I turned away and hooked my arm through Ricki's.

'Don't turn your back on me!' India grabbed my arm again, swinging me around. Ricki, her arm looped with mine, came along for the ride, her hair swooping out wildly.

'Wheeee!' she cried.

I unpeeled India's hand from my arm. 'And don't you touch me.'

'Ooh,' India said again, wobbling her head from side to side. 'Thinks she's better than us. Thinks she's the best rider in the school.'

'Wrong!' Ricki said, holding up her hand in a stop sign. 'She knows she's the best.'

I nudged her. That kind of comment wasn't going to help.

'You think you're so good,' India spat. 'But you're not. You're just some kid they felt sorry for.'

'I don't have to listen to this,' I said. I tugged on Ricki's arm. She was pointing her wand at India, like it was a sword, and making zapping noises.

'Yes, you do. When I ride here for seven years and don't get the riding scholarship, you have to listen to every word I say.'

'It's not my fault you didn't get it.'

I'd never been scared of India before, but things had changed after the last riding lesson with Demi. Demi hadn't said it outright, but I could see it in her eyes: if I didn't ride like a champion, and behave like one too, I could lose my scholarship. It would go to India instead, and there was no way I'd let that happen.

'I'll let up on you, on one condition,' India said. Her smile was radiant. She'd obviously planned something special for me. 'There's a horse here called Lightning — he's wild, unrideable.'

'So why's he at the school?'

'He's Demi's. He's like her mission in life. She reckons he could have got her to the Olympics, but it never happened. That's why she's always cranky.'

'What's this got to do with me?' My heart had started to thump. I knew what she was going to say before she even opened her mouth.

'If you can ride him, I'll leave you alone. Only the best rider in the school could stay on that horse, and the scholarship student is supposed to be the best, right?'

I thought about it. I could feel her watching me, biding her time. I knew she was hoping I'd mess up and be sent home for good.

'Don't do it, Ash.' Ricki was serious now.

I ignored her. 'You're on. When?'

'Any time between now and end of term,' India said. 'I can't wait.'

'Don't listen to her!' Ricki's eyes were wide. She tapped my head with her wand. 'You must be mad!'

I held out my hand and India shook it. 'Neither can I,' I said.

India smiled and turned away, disappearing into the crowd of Year Sevens who'd gathered to watch the lunchtime entertainment.

'Are you insane?' Ricki said. 'From the sounds of it, you could be killed by that horse. Or worse, lose your scholarship!' She poked her wand into her bag.

'I won't be killed. If I take my time, get to know him and give him treats … he'll start to like me. We've got five weeks 'til the end of term, right?'

Ricki nodded.

'I'll need a week or two to butter him up. I know — I'll do it after the polocrosse match. That way, if anything does go wrong, I won't be letting the team down.'

The bell rang. All around us, girls gathered their bags and began to make their way to their afternoon classes.

'Please don't do this,' Ricki said. She grabbed my hand. 'India's not worth it. Believe me, I know.'

This was the opportunity I'd been waiting for — to find out why India had tried to scare me away from Ricki. To find out what had happened between them in the past.

'What *do* you know?' I said. 'You have to tell me.'

Ricki shook her head. 'Not now. We'll be late.'

I looked around. The yard was nearly empty.

'Please!' I squeezed Ricki's hand but she grimaced.

'Some other time. Mrs Wright'll do unto us as the Romans did unto the rebel slaves in 71 BC.'

'We've got History now?'

Ricki pulled me towards the building. 'Why d'ya think I've been trying to hurry you up? That teacher's middle name is "lateness detention".'

I jogged after her. 'That's two middle names. How'd you remember that date, by the way?'

'Whaddya think I do when you're riding every afternoon?'

Ricki refused to say any more, but I knew she'd tell me at some point. I'd make sure of it. And I would win India's challenge. For me and for Ricki.

'All warmed up?' Maryanne James called, and waved me onto the polocrosse field. It had been newly lined and looked wonderful. I didn't feel too wonderful, though. It was my first training session with my team, the juniors, and I knew India was a Number Two. (I had fought to control my face when Maryanne had told me that!) There was only one plus: India could never ride in the goal-scoring area with me. I'd have to score as many goals as I could, just to steer clear of her.

I'd been named as a Number One. Maryanne had been so happy with my improved stick control that she'd decided to give me a go. Everyone knew that positions were never guaranteed. It was one of the coolest things about polocrosse. I could play all three positions in one match. It would never get boring!

I trotted Honey onto the field. She was as excited as I was and obviously chuffed with her fancy polocrosse tail-do. We'd trained on the field, either with the seniors, just with Maryanne or alone, every other day for weeks. It had been hard work for her and very demanding, but I'd watched her closely and she'd be well rested during the school holidays. I'd already decided not to take her home. She needed a break as much as I did and Linley was her home away from home now. I didn't want to disturb her routine all over again, and couldn't think of a better place for her to have some R and R. Besides, if my last weekend home was anything to go by, Becky and Pree probably wouldn't miss me on rides anyway.

'This is your team,' Maryanne said as I approached the five other riders on the field. 'India you know, of course.'

'Of course,' I said with a forced smile. India stared up at the sky, ignoring me.

'She's the only other Year Seven. This is Cleo Anderson on Dallas and Sarah De Silva on Pixie — they're Year Eights.'

'Hi,' said Cleo.

'Hot enough for ya?' asked Sarah.

I grinned at them, liking them instantly.

'And this is Katie Muir on Caramel and Stephanie Costa on Chops.'

'Year Nine?' I said.

They nodded.

Maryanne gave us our first team pep talk. It was going to be a big year for all of us. We had one match this term, a friendly. But the comp would hot up in second term with matches every other week. At the end of the season there would be a grand final and the tournament's champion team would be declared. The Linley Heights Juniors had missed out by one goal last season and Maryanne wasn't going to cop that again!

Next, Maryanne had us face each other, three per side, and practise catching and throwing at a halt, walk, trot and a canter. I missed a few balls — most often the ones thrown by India. In return, I made sure I flicked the ball so high above her head only Pegasus could have caught it. That aside, I managed pretty well overall. Maryanne gave me the thumbs up. She knew I was desperate to prove myself a worthy member of the team. Sometimes the other players resented the scholarship student's 'free ticket' onto the team. They didn't understand that if I'd been on a tennis or swimming or music scholarship I'd have been expected to represent the school in tennis or swimming or music. Same with riding.

We were split into two teams of three, each made up of a Year Seven, a Year Eight and a Year Nine. It was India, Sarah and Katie (the blue team for this match) against me, Cleo and Stephanie (the red team). Maryanne gave us blue or red netball-style bibs to wear over our tops. She was going to umpire and had hooked Bridget and Alysha into goal umpiring and scorekeeping. Alysha was playing with a goalpost (they were bendy, just in case of collisions) and waved madly when she saw me. I waved back, wishing I was training with her instead of India.

I was Number One, Cleo was Number Two and Stephanie was Number Three and team captain for the day. The blue team captain was Sarah, also playing Number Three. India was Number Two (I knew that already!) and Katie was Number One.

'Ready, teams?' Maryanne said. She held up an air horn. 'We'll use this so the horses get used to the noise. It might take a while, but better to do it now than at the match. Remember, it's just three weeks away.'

Maryanne cantered across the field and handed the air horn to Bridget, who was timekeeping.

Stephanie turned to us. 'If you guys do me one favour this year, it'll be kicking their butts, okay?'

I smiled. 'No worries.'

'Ashleigh, Maryanne tells me you're good, but if you need to know anything call a time out and I'll come over. Don't take any rubbish from Katie — she's a rough player and she'll try to get away with anything she can. India, I don't know.'

I rolled my eyes. India had made out like she was some kind of expert.

'And Sarah's pretty cool, but she's a left-hander so watch her stick. If you see her change racquet hands during the match you have to let me know. She's not allowed to do that, but she is allowed to pick up or catch the ball on the non-stick side of her horse. Don't get the two things mixed up.'

Bridget raised the air horn.

Stephanie held up a crossed-fingered hand. 'Good luck, guys!'

BLAST! Bridget started the match.

Honey shied suddenly and, unprepared, I fell. I saw her silver shoes flash as she cantered away. I lay on the field for a few moments, unhurt, but too stunned to move.

Maryanne was there in a heartbeat. 'What happened? Are you okay? Can you sit up?'

'Yeah, I'm okay.'

I sat up and looked for Honey, and saw with relief that Alysha was leading her back to me. My team-mates stared at me and then my horse.

'I think she shied at the air horn,' I said.

'She sure did!' Maryanne had dismounted and offered me her hand. 'Up you get.'

I stood up and felt a stinging in my arm. My elbow was bleeding and a long red streak had run down my arm. A fly wasted no time in buzzing around what it saw to be a feast.

Alysha handed me Honey's reins and I mounted. I knew I had to get up on her back straightaway. It was better for her and for me. I rubbed my hand on her shoulder, reassuring her that all was well.

'You right to play?' Maryanne was watching me carefully.

I nodded. I didn't want India to think I was weak. 'No problem.'

Bridget raised the air horn again. I prepared myself, keeping my hands close to the pommel just in case. I wasn't supposed to ride hanging on to it, but a good handful of pommel or mane could often help a rider stay on an out-of-control horse.

BLAST!

Honey shied again. This time I was ready. I sat as

deep as I could and clamped my legs to her middle. I grabbed the pommel and held on. Not satisfied with her leap to the left, Honey added a pig-root to the mix, then another. I took charge, wheeling her around to the right. I'd heard once that riding a horse in a tight circle could bring it under control. I only hoped it was true.

Maryanne was at my side again and grabbed Honey's bridle. My horse stopped, panting like a wild thing. She tossed her head back again and again and went into reverse — her favourite 'I don't like this' trick.

Maryanne dismounted, still gripping my bridle. She looked up at me. Her face was tight. 'You can't train on her today. Not if she's going to shy at the horn.'

'Just try her again,' I said. 'One more chance, please!'

I felt I'd gone back in time and was pleading my case at Waratah Grove to Alex, the dressage coach. He'd banished Honey from the arena. I did *not* want that to happen here at Linley.

I could see Maryanne was thinking hard. 'I dunno,' she said.

'Once more!'

'I could always just sub a horse for you.'

'But we've trained so hard. Please?'

I gave her the look I'd tried out on my first day at Linley Heights, on the school tour. It had worked then. But Maryanne hadn't been holding a terrified horse by the bridle that day.

'Last chance,' she said finally. 'But if she does it again, she's being subbed.'

Maryanne let go of Honey and I wheeled her in a circle again, small and tight. I watched Bridget. She raised the horn slowly.

BLAST!

Honey took off. She bolted across the polocrosse field, past India (who 'whoo-hooed') and Bridget, straight towards the fence. I tried to get her into the circle again. I'd need a wide circle this time — a tight one would see Honey on the ground, possibly on top of me. A wide circle was the best way to slow a bolting horse. Honey galloped closer to the fence. I squeezed my legs against her sides, trying to remind her I was there, and held my right rein out wide, as if I was opening a car door. I squeezed my left rein again and again. She ignored me, shaking her head and making for the fence. She wanted out.

I had no choice. It was go with her or hit the ground.

I gathered my reins and grabbed a huge handful of mane. Honey lifted off and sailed clear over the fence. She touched down on the other side. What now? There was the possibility she could jump a second fence and wind up in a paddock. I didn't want to be on the back of a bolting horse surrounded by a mob of riderless horses. No way!

I tried wheeling her again, holding my left hand at my hip and refusing to give, and this time she listened. In a minute I had her under control, in a nice canter. We slowed to a trot, then a walk. I halted her at last and scrambled from her back to the ground, my legs wobbling like a too-tall tower of blocks. I sat on the ground and buried my face in my hands, the full terror of the bolt finally hitting me. What if she hadn't stopped? What if I'd been hurt? I couldn't even go to my mum for a cuddle. She was hours away. I sat there in the middle of the field, holding on to Honey's reins and cried harder than I had in ages.

After a while someone tapped my shoulder. Maryanne gave me a weak smile and sat beside me, cross-legged. 'Whaddya say we sub her?'

I nodded and wiped at my nose with my sore arm. 'Okay.'

'I've sent Bridgey to tack up Mystery for you. Mysty's really quiet, really experienced. I've seen her with the primary kids. She stops beside the ball so they can pick it up.'

I gave her a wobbly smile. 'I just wanted to show I could do it. I just wanna be as good as them.'

'You are.' Maryanne nudged me. 'In fact, you're better! Most of those girls'd run at the first sign of trouble. You didn't. You never gave up!'

I shook my head and wiped my face with my hands. I didn't know what to say. My heart was only just starting to beat normally. I must have been on an adrenalin rush.

'Let's get back in there,' Maryanne said. 'We still have a match in three weeks!'

She got up and I did likewise. I pulled my reins over Honey's head, checked she was standing square and told her to be still. I mounted and followed Maryanne back to my team-mates, trying as hard as I could to keep my head held high. In fact, it was so high, I could barely see anything over my nose.

Mystery was tacked up and ready to be warmed up. Bridget led Honey away and I prepared Mystery for the match.

When Bridget got back, she raised the horn and blasted. I flinched, but Mystery was fine. She practically played the match for me — a perfect polocrosse pony. But it wasn't right. I felt empty and embarrassed.

At the end of the session, it was decided I would ride Mystery in the friendly match. Honey would stay home alone.

I went to see my horse afterwards. She was in the corral, untacked, rugged and munching on a haynet. I rubbed her face with my hand and laid my head on her back.

'Why?' I said. 'Why did you do that?'

So much of her past, her personality, was still unknown to me. I needed to do a little more investigating, find out exactly what Honey, formerly known as Argonaut, had been through. The Internet was the place to start, but I knew I wouldn't have time until the end of the year, during the long summer break. In the meantime, I had to face the fact that Honey and I wouldn't be playing polocrosse together at all this term.

eighteen

Busted

'How're you feeling?' Em asked me.

'Stiff, sore, sorry. A few other "S" words.' I patted Honey's back and double-checked my girth. I hadn't ridden her since the polocrosse training session and wasn't taking any chances.

It had been two days since my fall and I was still aching. And it wasn't just my butt — it was my pride too. India had made sure that everyone at Linley Heights heard about what had happened. The story got better with each retelling from what Em and Ricki told me. In the most recent version, I'd been airlifted off the polocrosse field after being given the kiss of life by India herself. The whole school was calling her a hero. I was calling her other, more colourful nouns.

'I am so hyped about this ride!' Ricki said. She looked it too. Even her hair was hyped. It was kind of floating around her head, as if it was full of static electricity.

It was a Saturday afternoon. Competitive sport was finished for the day and Ricki had been allowed to stay back and ride — brilliant! To make things extra wonderful, Em and I had been given permission to go to Ricki's house for dinner instead of choking down the Saturday night menu of sausages, boiled veggies and mashed potatoes. And after sampling Ricki's mum's cooking the week before, I couldn't wait. I only hoped they hadn't decided to order pizza!

I looked at Em. She was in disguise, wearing a Linley riding uniform, my white helmet and sunglasses so huge they concealed half her face. One whiff of Em being anywhere near a horse would bring Mercedes Phuong sniffing around like a bloodhound. She'd been blackmailed once with the mascara thing, but it was unlikely Em would get a second chance. It was disguise or don't ride and Em was desperate to ride.

As a new rider, Em was keen to catch, groom and tack up George on her own. As a once-rider, now more interested in turning dandelions into rosebushes with one wave of her magic wand, Ricki was content to let me practise my tacking-up skills on Mystery. I had no idea how good a rider Ricki was, but I was sure that Mystery would treat her well, whether she made the best transitions the world had ever seen or couldn't tell the horse's head from her backside.

I was taking my friends on a horseback tour of the riding centre followed by a little work in the arena. As soon as Mystery was ready, and Ricki had tamed her hair enough to put on her borrowed helmet, we mounted and made our way down School Paddock Lane.

We rode past the yard where Honey had been quarantined when she'd first arrived at Linley Heights, and the mares' paddock where she now lived with the humungous bay horse with the goggle-eyed fly mask. We rode further along the lane. I'd never come this far before — I'd never had to.

'You're doing well,' I said to Ricki.

'I wasn't bad,' she said. 'I won a prize for riding in Year Three, actually.'

242

'Wow!' I was impressed. 'Which one?'

'Most Improved Rider. India won the award for Integrity, if you can believe it.' Ricki sniffed contemptuously.

'They must have changed the criteria that year,' I said, mimicking the first time India McCray had ever spoken to me.

'Are you ever gonna fill us in?' I asked Ricki, wriggling a little in the saddle. Honey tossed her head as if to say, 'Hey, who's driving?'

'Fill you in on what?' she asked, her face scrunched up like a confused monkey.

'On this thing between you and India.' I watched her intently. We were riding at a walk along a quiet school lane and I trusted Honey enough to know that I could concentrate on Ricki for a while. 'I mean, why is she so ... well, like she is with you?'

I glanced at Em who was listening in hard.

Ricki rolled her eyes. 'Oh that?'

'Yes,' I said. 'That.'

Ricki shrugged. 'It was the whole horse thing. Couldn't stand to see anyone out-ride her.'

I was astonished. 'Is that it?'

Ricki grimaced. 'Some people just can't stand to lose, Ash.'

We rode further down the lane, past the geldings' paddock and turned left. In the distance were a series of what seemed to be private paddocks. I was keen to check them out. Usually only the most valuable horses were kept in private paddocks. Or the most dangerous.

'What's for dinner tonight?' I said.

Ricki beamed. 'Pizza! Dad's ordering ten. He told me to ask you what your favourite topping is.'

'Pizza?' I forced my face into a smile.

I mustn't have been very convincing because Ricki collapsed in giggles.

'Should see your face, Ash. We're not having pizza. Coz I told Mum how much you liked that lunch, she's gone crazy! When I left this morning she was up to her elbows in lamb kebabs and has already made a bucket of her special potato salad — oh guys, you'll love it. She's roasting chicken with these spices too, and doing my favourite dessert for you guys.'

My stomach growled just thinking about it. Em was rubbing hers as well.

'Ricki, I just want you to know that we're always available to come to your place for dinner,' I said.

'Just say the word,' Em added. 'It's no trouble, really.'

Ricki giggled, delighted.

'Guys!' I cried. 'Look!' I pointed to a paddock a hundred metres away. There was a lone black horse standing there watching us.

'Who's that?' Em stood up in her stirrups for a better look.

'Only one way to find out,' Ricki said. 'I reckon I can still trot. Shall I?'

'Impress us!' I said.

Ricki waggled her fingers over Mystery's neck. '*Abbalababbala*, worms and dry rot, make this fine pony called Mystery trot!'

She frowned. 'It's not working.'

I giggled. 'Leg aids are way more magical!'

Ricki squeezed her legs and Mystery trotted forward. 'Wheeee!' she cried.

Em, who was still well and truly wearing her L-plates, and I followed at a walk.

We stopped in front of the black horse's paddock. He stood by the fence, looking out at us like he was the king of the world and we should be on our knees. He tossed his head and snorted. I was bedazzled. He was pure black, not a spot of white anywhere on him. He was unrugged and his coat glistened like a jewel. His muscles rippled with even the slightest movement and his neck was gracefully arched. His tail looked like it was made from silk and his eyes were wide and intelligent. His feet were perfect and black. He stood at least 16 hands high. He was magnificent.

'Whaddya reckon, Ash?' Ricki said. 'Thoroughbred?'

'Close,' I said. 'Anglo-Arab.'

She wrinkled her nose. 'You think?'

'Yup. Look at the shape of his head, the straight profile — that's the thoroughbred in him, but he has the Arab body — fine but strong. And check out those Arab legs.'

'You win.'

'There's a nameplate on the gate,' Em said in a hushed voice. '*Lightning*.'

I nearly fell off Honey. (Again!) *This* was Lightning, the horse India had challenged me to ride. I'd been aware of the clock ticking on her challenge, and now I'd found him.

'Brilliant!' I said. 'How lucky is that? We weren't even looking for him and here he is.'

'Life's like that a lot, eh, guys?' Ricki mused. 'Could've been magic.'

'The magic's in *him*,' I said. 'Just look at him. No

wonder Demi won't get rid of him.' I slid to the ground and handed Ricki my reins.

'Why would she get rid of him?' Em was lost. 'Is this the horse you were telling me about? The wild one?'

'Yup,' I said.

'Get away from him then!' Em's voice was shrill. 'Before he hurts you!'

I reached my hand out to the stallion and touched the tip of his nose. His nostrils flared and he snorted.

'He won't hurt me,' I murmured. 'He's a good boy, aren't you, Lightning?'

He tossed his head some more, just little tosses, up and down, then stamped the ground with his nearside foreleg.

The paddock gate was padlocked, but I had to get in. I shook the post-and-rail fence, then slipped between the first and second rails.

'Are you nuts?' Em shrieked.

I was annoyed. 'Don't yell around horses, especially this one!'

'You shouldn't be in there,' she said more quietly. 'This whole thing with India is stupid. Why didn't you just tell her to get lost?'

'I couldn't,' I said, shrugging.

'Sure you could,' Ricki cried, throwing her hands up in the air.

Em groaned. 'You're better than this, Ash. You know what my mum always says? *If Joe Bloggs told you to jump off the Sydney Harbour Bridge, would you do it?*'

'The Harbour Bridge is one thing, horses are another. Don't worry.' I winked at Em. 'I'll be right.'

I stroked the stallion's nose again and again. I would calm this horse. I would ride him. And when I did, no one would ever question my being at Linley Heights again. Not India, not anybody.

'Good ride?' I asked my friends as we led the horses into the corral. We'd loosened their girths and they'd had a drink.

'Top fun,' Ricki said. 'Can't feel my butt, but.'

'That was so awesome.' Em sighed. She tied George's reins to one of the many loops of twine secured to the corral fence, dreamy-faced. 'When can we ride again?'

'Just say the word.' I unbuckled Honey's girth and let it drop gently under her tummy, then stepped cautiously behind her, my hand running around her rump as I went, picked up the girth on the other side and laid it over the saddle. 'Next time we'll disguise you as Elvis.'

'Hilarious.' Emily rubbed George's forelock. His head drooped in pleasure. 'Now listen, I have a few words to say about that dumb challenge.'

'I'll show India,' I said. 'You just wait.'

'I'd be happy to wait,' Em said. 'As in forever. There's still time to call the whole thing off. No one will think badly of you if you do.'

'No way.' I rubbed at Honey's damp coat with an old towel. Her saddle was hung carefully on the fence and her saddle blanket was airing beside it. 'I'd never be able to look her in the face again.'

'What d'you care what she thinks?'

'We've been through this a gazillion times. Nothing you can say will change my mind. Okay?' I gave Em a look over Honey's back.

She shrugged. 'Excuse me for caring what happens to you. Sorry if I don't want to see you wrapped up like a mummy with a hundred broken bones.'

I smiled. 'You're a good mate, Em. Just promise me you'll be there cheering me on.'

Em took off her sunglasses and hooked them on the Linley Heights Junior Riding Team polo shirt she was wearing. They were so huge she'd been able to wear her normal glasses underneath. She frowned. 'I'll be there all right. But I won't be cheering.'

We rugged the horses and took them to their private stalls for feeding. It was the best fun, just laughing and talking and watching the horses eat. Until we heard the screech.

At first I thought it was India. Then I recognized the cropped black hair and my heart began to pound. Mercedes Phuong had found us.

'What are you doing here?' she barked, putting her face so close to her sister's that Em recoiled. 'Have you been riding?'

Em shook her head and looked at me. 'No, no, I—'

'You're lying!' Mercedes raged. 'Look at your pants. They're covered with horsehair. And your face is filthy. Do you really think I'm so stupid I wouldn't notice?'

Ricki nudged me and we exchanged glances, agreeing that Murky probably was that stupid.

'She didn't go far,' I said. 'I just led her around a bit.'

Mercedes's eyes popped. She stared so hard at me I thought she was having some kind of fit. It was pretty obvious that she wasn't used to being argued with by a twelve year old. It was even more obvious that she'd better get used to it!

'Whaddya mean, you just led her around?'

I shrugged. 'I mean, I begged her to come and wouldn't take no for an answer. She told me she wasn't allowed but I wouldn't let up. It's my fault. Don't tell your mum, please?'

'I'll do whatever I like,' she snapped. 'And you!' She turned on Emily. 'Get back to your room and clean yourself up.'

'But I'm going to Ricki's for dinner. Miss Stephens okayed it and every—'

'Not any more, you're not.'

'Mercedes!' Em wailed. 'That's not fair.'

'Get going,' Murk spat. 'Or I'll tell Mum you took off without permission as well.'

Em gave Ricki and me a weak smile. 'Sorry. Please tell your mum I—'

'Don't worry about it,' Ricki said with a shrug. 'I'll send something back with Ash.'

'I can't go if Em can't,' I said.

Emily shook her head. 'You have to go. What about all those souvlakis?'

I glanced at Ricki, torn. Her mum had been cooking all day. But Em was in trouble. I felt like

I was never there for her when she needed me. I'd talked her into wearing that sheet before our exeat, then left her to fend for herself when she got into trouble. And here I was on the verge of doing it again. What kind of friend was I?

'I won't go without you!' I said.

Ricki looked hurt. I felt like a double traitor.

Em grabbed my arm and hissed in my ear, 'You're going. And you're gonna have a good time. Don't worry about me. Just look at Ricki's face.'

I nodded. 'Okay. I'll see you when I get back. Just take care, all right?'

Em waved her hand like it was nothing, then followed her sister back towards the school. I felt like I'd swallowed a horseshoe and now it was clunking in the pit of my stomach. How could I enjoy a feast with Ricki knowing that Em was choking down sausages, boiled veggies and mashed potatoes? How could I laugh knowing that Em was crying?

Ricki hooked her arm around mine. 'She'll be okay.'

'I hope so,' I said.

I watched as Em disappeared from view, wishing I could make everyone happy.

Ricki and I groomed and turned out the horses, then ran to the school gates where her dad was waiting in his ute. He was nice, and I knew Ricki was proud to bring me into her home, but despite the delicious food and how warm Ricki's family were I couldn't wait to get back to Linley. I had a horrible feeling that something bad had happened to Em.

I crept up to her door on my way to bed and crushed my ear up hard against it. Was she okay? Was she awake? Was she still there or had her parents charged down from Barton as fast as their sleek four-wheel drive could carry them and whisked her back to the safety of a horse-free-future-lawyer existence?

I tapped on the door with my fingernail.

'Em?' I hissed. 'Em, are you asleep?'

Silence. I tried the doorknob but it was locked. I stood there for a moment and prayed as hard as I could to the horse gods. *Let her be okay. I'll cop the blame, but please let Em be okay.*

nineteen

Fallout

'Don't you wanna know what happened at Mum's meeting with Mr Sinclair?'

I rolled over in bed, tangled in my sheets, and pulled some hair out of my mouth. It was the morning after the dinner at Ricki's, and the room was flooded with light. I usually woke up in the dark, while Claire was still flat on her back fast asleep with her mouth wide open. I was going to have to break it to her eventually that sleeping like that just about guaranteed a nocturnal spider diet.

'What time is it?' I asked.

Claire looked at her perfectly neat desk where her school-issue digital clock stood perfectly aligned with her pens and pencils. I couldn't even find my clock under all the mess that had been piling up on my desk since my first day at Linley Heights. 'Eight forty-three,' she said.

I sat bolt upright. 'I slept in? Why didn't you wake me up?'

Claire smiled and batted her eyelashes. 'You looked so peaceful, like a little baby. I just didn't have the heart.'

I was out of bed in a nanosecond, riffling through the clothes on my section of the floor for my least filthy joddies. 'I'll be late for polocrosse practice!'

'Oh, what a shame,' Claire said, tutting. 'While you're at it, can't you clear up all that disgusting muck? I can't live like this any longer. I've told my mother everything and she said she'd go to Mrs Freeman about it.'

'Good,' I said, pulling on a boot and trying to shake some mud onto Claire's side of the room. 'While she's at it, maybe she can tell her what a total pain you are to live with.'

'You'd better watch yourself,' Claire said. 'Don't forget my mum's the president of the Parents' Association.'

'How could I?' I muttered. I stamped my way into my other boot and rummaged through my drawer for a shirt, tearing at my hair with a fuzzy old brush.

'Are you at least gonna clean your teeth?' Claire said.

'No time.' I pulled a polo shirt over my head. 'Why don't you let me give 'em a polish with your pillowcase?'

Claire went pale. 'Mum's meeting with Mr Sinclair went really well,' she said, answering her own question.

I yawned, and twisted my hair into a messy ponytail.

'It was just like I said. He hated the horses before and he hates them now. He said he'd give Mum his full support.'

She made me so mad. It had been terrible enough not knowing how Em was, and having to go to Ricki's without her. I'd had a great time and feasted on the most delicious food I'd eaten in weeks, but it would have tasted even better if all three of us had been together. And now it looked as if stupid Claire might get her way about the riding program.

'Support this!' I wiggled my bottom at Claire and stormed out of the room, slamming the door as hard as I could behind me. (As it had one of those slow-closing devices screwed into it, to prevent squished fingers, it didn't slam as well as I'd hoped.)

I ran as fast as I could, scummy teeth, no breakfast and all, to the riding centre. The practice had been scheduled for eight-thirty. Maryanne had probably already decided to have me strapped to a goalpost and flogged with a polocrosse stick. I didn't know how well that would work, with the goalposts being all bendy, but I was sure she'd have worked out a backup plan.

Mystery was there in the corral, tacked up and waiting. Someone kind had already tied up her tail for me. I half-smiled, half-cursed. I'd wanted to ride Honey in the match so badly. I'd accepted that we wouldn't make our debut as a team just yet, but accepting it didn't mean I had to like it.

I tightened Mystery's girth and stretched her legs, making sure there were no flaps of skin caught underneath that might pinch, then untied her reins frantically. I could hear the whoops from the polocrosse pitch. It was time to warm up and get into the action.

By the time I'd warmed Mystery up, the juniors were well into their training session. Maryanne's face was purple when she turned to watch me canter onto the field.

'You're late!' she hissed. 'We've already warmed up and done all our catching and throwing practice.'

I wriggled into the red bib that Cleo Anderson flicked at me from the pitch and accepted the stick that Maryanne thrust into my face. 'I know. Sorry, I—'

'No excuses for lateness!' Maryanne said. She wheeled Cav in a tight circle, brandishing a stick of her own. She wouldn't use it to play, but needed it for her umpire's signals. I was just getting to know what they all meant, but the one I most wanted to see was a stick held straight up in the air. That meant one thing. Goal!

'What if the school was burning down and I was guiding all those poor teachers to safety?' I said, gathering both reins in my left hand and holding the racquet tightly in my right. 'What if I stopped to help an old lady cross the road? What if a kangaroo hopped right up to me and tried to tell me there was a little kid clinging to a cliff face and—'

'Enough!' she snapped. But there was a hint of a smile tugging at her lips. A very small hint. 'At least you're in time for the first chukka.'

I asked Mystery for a trot, squeezing my legs and giving with my left hand, and the grey pony responded, heading straight for the action. I should have been here, warming up with my team. It was all that business with Em. I hadn't slept well because of worrying about her, and then when I did fall asleep, I'd overslept.

'Ready, teams?' Maryanne hollered. Cav turned another few circles as we lined up side by side, red, blue, red, blue …

BLAST!

The air horn bellowed and the game was on. Maryanne threw the ball in. Everyone reached up with their sticks at once. It was like synchronized sticking! Katie snatched at the ball but missed and it hit the ground with a thump. The pack attacked it and, after some sort of horseback ruck, Sarah De Silva held up her stick, the ball balanced on the racquet. She needed to get moving fast, but I cut her off.

'Hey!' she cried.

I grinned. 'Sorry!'

Stephanie Costa whacked Sarah's stick upwards and the ball went flying — ZIP!

'I'm gonna get you, Costa!' Sarah shrieked.

'Yee-haw!' Stephanie turned Chops towards the goal and looked over her shoulder for me. 'Giddup, Ash!'

I cantered alongside her. We were ten metres from the penalty line, then five, then one.

'Now!' She flicked me the ball. 'Score, you're clear!'

The blue goal was undefended. The blue Number Three was being very irresponsible! I leaned forward to scoop, but missed. The ball landed to our right, a few metres away.

'Get it!' Stephanie cried.

Mystery spun around. 'Whoa!' I clung to the pommel — something I tried not to do too much of, but I was on board a revolving horse!

She stopped dead in front of the ball, almost pointing to it.

Easy, I thought, leaning over to scoop.

'Think quick!' Katie Muir said, appearing from out of nowhere and snatching it up.

I felt useless. The odds had never been so good for a goal, but I'd missed the ball, then lost it.

'I'll get it,' Stephanie said, looking annoyed. 'You get into the goal-scoring area.'

'I can help!' I said, almost pleading. It hadn't been my fault — I mean, I hadn't set out to miss the ball. But it had happened and I wanted to right my wrong. And save face in front of my team. I was on a mission to redeem myself.

I watched Stephanie zoom away after Katie. Cleo closed in as well and sticks flew. I cantered Mystery to our team's goal.

'Good of you to finally show up!'

It was India, hard on Mystery's heels.

'What're you doing here?' I sneered. 'Aren't you a great big Number Two?'

'Funny.' India didn't look amused. 'You obviously still don't know the rules of the game. I can play any position as long as—'

I rolled my eyes. 'I know the rules.'

'Coulda fooled me.'

I ignored her and focussed on the action.

'Here, Cleo, HERE!' Stephanie bellowed.

Cleo had scooped up the ball from between Sarah and Katie and was looking around frantically for support. Stephanie charged for the red team's goal, ready to defend it.

Cleo's eyes flashed. 'Thanks for being here, guys!'

She held the stick out in front of her, away from the blue team. Dallas, knowing what was required of him, burst into a gallop. In only a few seconds Cleo was nearing the penalty line. I readied myself for the catch, holding Mystery back. She danced underneath me, desperate to tear away.

India cut in front of me, screeching at her teammates. It was going to be a showdown between India and me — we were the only two players allowed in the goal-scoring area. I would rather eat the ball than see India with it in her racquet.

I made a quick decision. Whether Stephanie approved or not, I was going to take a chance.

I cantered Mystery past India and over the penalty line. It was risky moving too far from the goal-scoring area, but I knew she'd never let up. I had to trap her and Rusty. If I could only block them in, I'd be okay.

'Ash, where ya going?' Cleo screamed.

I cantered fast towards the blue team goal and called out to Stephanie. We didn't need her defending. Blue had no chance of scoring.

I heard the thunder of hooves behind me and peered over my shoulder. It had worked! India was on my tail, just where I wanted her to be.

Stephanie watched me canter past, her mouth open. India was gaining on me, faster and faster. I knew she wanted me as far away from the goal-scoring area as possible. Light years away if she could manage it. I was closer and closer to the red goal, further and further from the blue. India was breathing down my joddies. Rusty was nose to tail with Mystery. That's when I asked her to halt.

I squeezed hard with my legs and pulled back on the reins.

'Whoa!' I cried.

She halted at once. If I hadn't been expecting it, I would have gone flying over her head and SPLAT onto the field. I wheeled her around.

India, in shock, lost her balance. For a second my heart stopped beating, fear that she'd fall ripping through my guts. I couldn't stand her, but I didn't want her to get hurt.

I watched her over my shoulder as I cantered Mystery back down the field towards Cleo, who was tearing around, the precious ball inside her racquet, which she was holding as high above her head as she could while staying within the rules.

India recovered her seat and brought Rusty around sharply.

'Now, Steph!' I screeched. 'Go get 'er!'

Stephanie Costa knew what I wanted her to do. She made a dash for India and blocked her.

No matter which way India tried to turn, duck or weave, Steph was there. Not even Houdini himself could have ridden his way out of Steph's web. I whooped with joy. If I could just make it to the goal-scoring area alone, with the ball in my racquet, we'd score for sure.

'Hurry, Ash!' Cleo yelled. She turned hard right and drew her arm back, stood up in her stirrups and flicked the ball to me.

I prayed as hard as I could to the horse gods. *Let me catch this ball, just this one ball.*

I could feel Maryanne's eyes stripping me to the bone. She'd given up so much time to help me train. If I missed this one, she'd have my guts for girth straps!

The ball soared and kinked left. I was going to miss it! Mystery seemed to be reading my mind. I could have sworn that horse knew where the ball would land — a touch from my legs and a tug from my hand and she was under it. All I had to do was hold out my stick.

I wanted to cry with relief when the ball landed in my net with a gentle ZOOP. There was no time for tears, though. India may have been totally blocked in by some of the best riding I'd ever seen (good one,

Steph!), but Sarah De Silva and Katie Muir were out for blood. Well, out for the ball anyway.

Their eyes locked in on my stick. Their horses locked in on Mystery. They rode side by side towards me, a move I knew was meant to freak me out, make me mess up.

Cleo cut in front of them but it was no use. It was code red and they were about to unleash operation block and score.

I knew they'd attack, no matter which way I went. One would hit my stick while the other scooped up the ball. With Stephanie still distracted and Cleo riding around in circles, I had no defence.

There was a crack of space between my attackers. Enough to squeeze through an undernourished alpaca but certainly not a 13-hands-high grey pony mare with a twelve year old (holding up a polocrosse stick) on board.

I had 1.35 seconds to think. I would do what they least expected me to do.

I would ride through them.

They were dead ahead. I gathered my reins in my left hand and sat deep in the saddle, leaning slightly forward and gripping my stick handle so hard I could feel my fingernails digging into my palm.

I squeezed hard with my legs.

'Go, Mysty!' I cried.

The mare leaped into a canter, straight at them. They looked at me, then each other, then panicked and wheeled away in opposite directions, giving me a clear path home. Mystery and I raced to the goalposts. I raised my stick and flicked and the ball soared through.

Maryanne held her stick straight up in the air, the signal that a goal had been scored, and the red team cheered.

I slowed Mystery to a trot, then a walk, rubbing her neck with my hand and praising her. She was the best, the best!

Then I felt guilty. How could I think that about another horse? Honey was my best, my only horse. I shook my head, trying to force all the bad thoughts out through my ears. My nostrils, even.

'Top riding, Ash!' Maryanne shouted, stopping Cav in front of me.

'Whoo-hoo!' Cleo cantered across and held up her hand. We high-fived.

'Good job!' Stephanie yelled, joining the celebrations.

'Let's hope you ride like that against the other

team on Saturday,' Katie said, rubbing at a splodge of mud on her face.

I beamed at them all. This was so wonderful, so fantastic. I loved this game. I couldn't believe I'd gone through my entire horsy life and never played it until now.

'Linley Juniors rock!' Sarah cried.

We were a team.

It was lunchtime and I was starving. After the match (red team five goals to blue team two!) I cooled down, groomed and turned out Mystery, then checked on Honey only to discover a huge raw bite on her neck and one on her rump. I'd expected a few scuffles while the horses in the paddock sorted out the new pecking order — maybe a lump or a bump — but nothing like this, especially under her rug. I instantly suspected Fly Eyes, but Honey looked like she'd done ten rounds with a great white! Chunks of her gorgeous bronze-coloured coat had been sliced away, but thankfully the skin wasn't broken and she wasn't bleeding. It didn't look like she was having any fun in that paddock at all.

I cursed as I applied a thick healing cream to the sores. I made up my mind to ask Joe for a new home for Honey, which was exactly what I did the second I caught a glimpse of him. After a bit of wailing and teeth-gnashing (from me, not Joe), we had a deal. One more bump or bruise and Honey would move in with the ponies.

'She'll be paddock mates with Mystery!' I squealed, delighted.

'Maybe,' Joe grumbled. 'Don't count your fillies, Ash.'

I watched Fly Eyes's every move for a while, then, after promising Honey I'd be back to stand guard, I bolted up to the dining room for lunch.

'It's only starvation that's making me eat this,' I said, dropping into the seat opposite Em and slapping my plate on the table. My fishcakes jiggled and my peas rolled around the plate. 'Is it just me or is the food only good when the parents are around?'

Em stared hard at her lunch. It was hardly touched and looked cold.

'Em? Are you okay?'

Emily said nothing. She picked up her plate, scraped out her chair and walked away, crossing the room to what we'd always called the Old Girls' side. Then she sat down at an empty table and put her face in her hands.

I was shocked. So shocked my face went numb. What had I done?

I followed her to her new table and sat opposite her again.

'What's wrong?' I said. I was practically begging. 'What happened? Are you okay?'

Em was silent, refusing to look at me. Her face was still covered by her hands.

I touched her hand and tried to peel her fingers away. She got up and walked away again, this time without her plate, weaving through the tables and out of the dining hall. I was on my way after her when a taller girl with cropped straight black hair stepped in front of me.

'Stay away from my sister.'

I looked up at Mercedes Phuong. 'Nice mascara.'

Her face reddened, but she didn't budge. 'Did you hear me? I said stay away. You'll only make things worse.'

'Why?' I said, trying to get past her. My friend needed me and her bird-brained big sister was coming between us again.

'I told Mum everything. She agrees with me that you're a bad influence.' Mercedes looked triumphant. 'She told Emily that if she so much as looks at you again she'll be out of Linley Heights before you can say "horse riding"!'

'You're a … a …' I couldn't find a word to describe her. It was as if she wanted Em to get into trouble, as if she was trying to earn points or something.

'I'm a what?' Mercedes's eyes narrowed and her lips thinned out.

'You're a creep!'

I pushed past her and ran from the dining hall, no longer hungry, just sick and scared. Very scared.

'Em!' I cried. 'Em, where are you?'

I ran down the corridor towards her room. Someone grabbed my arm and pulled me into the boarders' lounge. Em stuck her hand over my mouth. Her face was red and streaked with tears. 'Shush. She's probably after me already.'

I nodded and Em peeled her hand from my mouth. 'But why? We weren't doing anything wrong, we just—'

'Ash, are you my friend?' Em's eyes were wide.

I nodded. 'Of course. With all my heart.'

She grabbed my hands and looked into my eyes. 'Then stay away. I need you to do that for me. My parents never make empty threats.'

'Can't you go to Mrs Freeman — tell her everything?'

Em shrugged. 'What's Mrs Freeman gonna do? Mum and Dad have the right to send me to school here or take me away. Besides, it's not gonna help your anti-Carlson campaign if my lot show up and complain about me horse riding, is it?'

I shook my head, miserable.

'I'm still your friend, and you're mine. But we can't be together any more. Not like we were.' Em gulped and the tears flowed. She slipped her glasses off and rubbed them on her T-shirt.

'But why?' I just didn't understand.

'I don't wanna leave Linley, Ash. I might not be allowed to talk to you, but at least I know you're here. The horses too.'

I didn't agree, but I got it. I drew Em into a tight hug, knowing it could be the last time I was close enough to her to tell her anything. 'You're a top mate,' I said. I meant to say more. But it's hard to get those sorts of words out around a huge lump in your throat.

Em broke away and waved. 'Bye, Ash. Kiss Georgie boy for me. Tell him I'll never forget him.'

271

I nodded and wiped at the tears that were spilling down my face. It wasn't fair. It just wasn't fair.

Em ran from the room. I collapsed in a lounge chair and sobbed. I didn't care who saw me or heard me or what they thought. I'd lost my new friend and my heart was hurting.

twenty

Polocrosse Magic

'All set?' Ricki said.

I nodded, pulling my white Linley Heights polocrosse helmet onto my head.

'You look great.'

Ricki bobbed around me, so excited she'd forgotten the words of the magic spell she'd been trying to cast over me. I prayed to the horse gods that *Ibbilly bibbilly milkshakes and more, this spell will help Ashleigh ride good and sore — oops ... sorry, Ash, I meant 'good and score'!* was completely ineffectual.

I admired myself in the changing room mirror. It was an away game, and for the sake of my spotlessly clean polocrosse uniform I'd decided to pack everything into a gear bag and get dressed at the field. I was glad I had. So far I'd tripped over a tree root, shovelled at least three bags of horse poo, and managed to smear icky hoof contents all over myself while cleaning out Mystery's feet.

Now, though, I was wearing my new pair of breathtakingly white joddies, a blue polo shirt with Linley Heights Junior Polocrosse Team embroidered on the front and I'd polished my riding boots especially. A huge plastic Number One had been slipped into the envelope on the back of my shirt. I twirled my stick. I looked good. I felt great!

'Wish me luck!' I said, grabbing Ricki's hand with my stick-free hand. I was nervous. If I concentrated really hard on something else — like how I hadn't spoken to Em in a whole week, or how I had a Geography skills test coming up, or how I still couldn't play 'Twinkle Twinkle Little Star' on the violin, or how the Lightning challenge had been set for that very afternoon — I was able to forget about the match. But only for a moment and then my tummy started churning again and I sweated and shook and felt sick and wished I could just go home and get into bed. Maybe I was using the wrong strategy. Maybe thinking about all those totally horrible things wasn't working. I tried to think about doughnuts with pink icing and green sprinkles instead, but all that did was make me hungry. Hungry and sick, which was a bad feeling. A very bad feeling indeed.

Ricki hugged me quickly and ran for the polocrosse field. She had a surprise for me, she'd said, and had to get it ready. I took one last look at myself, zipped up my gear bag, slung it over my shoulder and left the changing room. It was show time.

'We're two goals down and there's no way I want to see Wallaby Hill score one more point. Do I make myself clear?' Maryanne James was red-faced and shaking.

'Yes, sir!' I cried.

My team laughed. All except India, of course. She rolled her eyes and mouthed 'loser' at me.

'I mean, it, Ash,' Maryanne said, nodding towards the pink-shirted Wallaby Hill Junior Polocrosse Team, who were in their between-chukka huddle. 'They flogged us last year fifteen to three. I don't care if this is a friendly match, Wallaby Hill ain't a real friendly bunch. So let's give it to 'em!'

'Woo, woo, woo!' Sarah cried, punching the air.

It was chukka five. Two more to go until the end of the match. Polocrosse games could be anywhere from six to eight chukkas but with a full schedule of friendlies to play that day the State Polocrosse Association had decided six was enough. The score was five-three, Wallaby Hill's way. We had sixteen minutes to right a wrong. Sixteen minutes to save Maryanne James from humiliation at the sticks of the Wallabies.

It was my turn to sit out. I remained, mounted at the side of the field, cheering and screaming as the ball was thrown in and Sarah, playing Number One, charged forward on Pixie, swiped at it with her stick and collected it, then made a mad dash for goal, shooting and scoring before I'd taken a breath, a pack of pink on her tail.

Five-four.

I held my stick under my arm and chewed on my thumbnail. Watching was no fun — I wanted to be out there. From the sideline I could see where Linley should go, what Wallaby Hill were up to, but I couldn't help. All I could do was wait for the eight-minute chukka to be over.

The crowd roared. Wallaby Hill had scored again. Their Number One rode a victory lap, winking at me as she flew past. I gritted my teeth. It was that or sink them into my own skin.

Six-four.

The teams lined up and the umpire threw in the ball. India stretched up. Although part of me wanted to see her miss, I was relieved when she caught it. She was Number Two again, and had to get the ball to Sarah or Katie who could get it over the penalty line. The Wallabies surrounded her. She had a thin strip of field and a mass of pink shirts in her face.

Sarah cantered away from the pack. 'Here, India!' she screamed.

India raised her stick and flicked the ball. It soared over the Wallabies' heads and Sarah swiped at it. The Wallabies turned and swarmed on Sarah and the ball. There was a mess of sticks and horses and legs and helmets and then the pink shirts had the ball. They whooped and cantered for their goal, flicking it between them as if they were toying with us, then their Number One shot for goal. Again.

The crowd shrieked and the air horn blasted. The chukka was over. The score was seven-four.

Chukka six, the last eight minutes of the match, and I was back on and goal-scorer. My whole body shook.

'Nice riding,' I said as India joined our huddle.

'Let's see you do better,' she spat.

My mouth hung open. I'd meant it. She'd played well. I didn't want to fight with her during our matches. All that business was going to be resolved at the Lightning Challenge that afternoon. But there wasn't time to argue. We had a minute to discuss strategy and the game was back on.

'Get 'em, Ash!' someone screamed. I twisted around. It was Ricki. She was holding up a huge banner that said *LINLEY JUNIORS TO WIN!* So that was the surprise. I hoped she was right. My heart squeezed as I thought about Em and how she should be here too.

I trotted Mystery onto the field, rubbing her neck with my stick-hand. 'We've gotta do this, Myst. We've gotta win!'

The umpire called for the line-up and I took my place beside a pink shirt, the Wallaby Hill Number One. My rival. My sworn enemy.

'You've got no chance, Linley girl,' she hissed.

I glared at her. When the words came out they made me sound much more fearsome than I felt. 'You wanna bet?'

The ump had the ball in her hand. She held it up.

BLAST!

The air horn howled and the last chukka was on.

The ump threw in the ball and there was a jostling of horses, arms and sticks. The Wallaby beside me scooped it up and I reached over, hitting her stick up hard. The ball flew out again.

'You!' she gasped. Then she said a lot of bad words.

The umpire appeared. 'Penalty, Wallaby Hill.'

'What?' I said. 'She swore!'

'Didn't hear a thing. But I did see you reach over her horse's neck to hit her stick.'

The umpire cantered away and the ball was presented to Wallaby One.

She smiled at me as she prepared to take her shot. 'Gets 'em every time!'

I raged inside. She'd deliberately stirred me up. She'd wanted me to be angry. She'd known I'd do something stupid.

'Good one, Ashleigh!' India called.

I didn't look at her. I didn't like her, but she hadn't cost us a penalty. I was the only one who'd managed to do that.

Wallaby One's team positioned themselves. It was going to be almost impossible to stop them scoring. Their Number Two was blocking Cleo and their Number One was waiting in the goal area. Like they expected it to be easy.

Wallaby One raised her stick, as if she was going to flick the ball. Linley prepared, raising their own sticks, me included. But then she burst into a canter and belted towards the goal. I was so shocked I didn't react at first. Then I touched Mystery's sides and tore after her. She'd got me once. I wasn't going to let it happen again. I had to block her. I had to stop her getting to goal. And I had to get that ball.

Cleo and Stephanie joined in the chase. The Wallaby Number Two followed as well, cutting her horse across in front of Cleo. Cleo was quick and turned Dallas left as the Wallaby cut right, and the Wallaby was left far behind.

Wallaby One was half a body length in front of me, then a nose. The goal was just ahead. She swung her stick back and I reached over, nowhere near her horse's neck this time, and hit up with everything I had. The ball hit the ground.

Mystery slowed to a trot, but the Wallaby kept on cantering. It was as if it had happened so fast she hadn't realized the ball was gone. Cleo swooped in and collected the ball, then turned Dallas for goal. Steph rode on her right side, I rode on her left. There was no way Wallaby Hill was getting anywhere near her stick.

We had until the penalty line to make the switch.

'Ready, Ash?' Cleo panted.

I broke away, forward. Cleo bounced the ball from her stick to the ground. The Wallaby Three pounced but I was too fast. Steph came to the rescue and cut Wallaby Three off while I bolted for the goal, swinging my arm back and letting fly.

It was in!

Seven-five.

'You played well,' Maryanne announced at the end of the match.

'We didn't win,' India grouched, and gave me a look. 'I wonder why?'

'We didn't win,' Maryanne said, 'but we finished the game on seven-six. We scored a last-minute goal and Wallaby Hill didn't score once in that last chukka. That's a sure sign of great teamwork!'

'Are you serious?' I asked.

Maryanne nodded. 'You guys never stopped fighting. You never gave up. They're a tough team, and seven-six is way better than fifteen-three, wouldn't you say?'

I smiled, feeling for the first time like a real polocrosse player. I'd had the most amazing time and the best fun. I only wished that Mum, Dad, Jase, Jenna, Becky, Pree and Em had been here to see me. At the thought of Becky my heart tightened. I hadn't called her. Here I was thinking myself brave enough to take on the Lightning Challenge and I hadn't been brave enough to call my best friend, not even once. Pree's emails and texts had kept me going, and kept me up to date on what was happening in Shady Creek. But Becky's silence hurt more than anything. Would things be better by the holidays? I was going home for Easter and I didn't want to spend two weeks alone, horseless and friendless.

I shook my head to clear it of sad thoughts, and joined the others in cooling out, untacking, grooming and rugging our horses. We untied their tails, fitted their tail guards and replaced their exercise and coronet boots with travel boots. We gave them a drink and let them rest before loading them into the Linley Heights horse truck. Then we clambered inside and headed for home.

It had been an incredible morning. And the day was about to get better. The Lightning Challenge was on that afternoon and I was ready to show India I was just as good as her. Ready to face my fears head on and conquer them. This was my chance to put any doubts about my scholarship to bed forever.

twenty-one

Lightning Strikes

A crowd had gathered at Lightning's paddock. It seemed that almost every boarder was crammed into the tiny lane — India had done a good job of spreading the word. Apart from Em and Ricki, I hadn't told a single person. I scanned the faces — Emily was nowhere to be seen, not even in disguise. I'd hoped so much that she'd come. I needed her now more than ever.

'I've got a message for you,' Ricki hissed at me over the fence. 'It's from Emily. She said don't do this. She wishes she could come and stop you herself.'

I nodded, almost unable to speak. 'Th-thanks.' My teeth were chattering and my whole body shook.

Ricki looked desperate. 'Please, just call it off.'

I shook even harder and looked at the crowd — dozens and dozens of Linley girls. 'I can't.'

Lightning was jumpy. He wasn't used to company, especially this many people. Over the last few weeks I'd spent as much time as I could stroking his nose and feeding him treats, but it didn't seem to have made much difference. I'd tacked him up in Honey's gear and was doing my best to calm him. His nostrils flared as he breathed hard in and out. His eyes rolled back and he pulled hard on the reins. I was barely managing to keep hold of his head.

'Good luck then,' Ricki said. She was nearly in tears. 'I'll be here. I'm staying with you.'

India stood up on the lower rail of the fence. 'Ladies and … well, ladies. Welcome to this afternoon's challenge.'

The crowd whooped.

Lightning reared, his forelegs thrashing. I gave him his head, but held fast to the reins, trying to stand as clear as I could. He was only on his hind legs for a few seconds but it felt like hours. I had been nervous before, but now I was petrified.

'Ashleigh Miller will now attempt to ride Lightning the Wild Horse!' India shouted, in her element. 'If she stays in the saddle for one minute, she will be declared worthy.'

I shuddered.

'But if she falls before the sixty seconds are over, she will leave Linley Heights forever!'

'What?' I was horrified. 'That was never part of the deal. You said if I rode him you'd leave me alone.'

'Read the fine print,' India said, laughing.

'I'm not leaving Linley,' I said. 'I don't care what happens.'

India smirked at me, then tipped back her head and opened her mouth. 'Ride the Wild Horse!' she yelled.

The girls screamed and jumped up and down.

Lightning shrieked with terror and spun around.

I clung to his reins, falling to the ground. I could hear laughter. I scrambled to my feet, knowing Lightning could crush me, knowing how utterly stupid I'd been to agree to this. Emily was right. She was a true friend. Nothing India had said should have mattered this much.

I pulled down on the reins and flicked them quickly over the stallion's head. He tossed his head over and over, stamping his nearside foot. His nostrils were red. He reared again and the reins were torn from my hands.

'Horsewoman of the Year!' India screeched.

Lightning touched down and I took my chance. He was enormous. I needed a mounting block, but there was nothing I could use in his paddock. I'd just have to wriggle my way onto his back. I reached up to the pommel and gripped tight with my left hand, clamping my right to the back of the saddle. I wasn't tall enough to reach further over. I just hoped I'd tightened the girth enough to stop it from sliding under Lightning's belly as I tried to mount.

'Quiet! Everyone quiet!' That was Ricki.

The girls settled and Lightning seemed to settle with them. I reached up to the stirrup with my left foot and bounced with my right, hauling myself up onto his back. Then I was there, looking down at his head, at the back of his sleek black ears. I reached out gingerly and touched his neck, rubbing gently to let him know I was pleased. Then I adjusted my seat slowly, so slowly, found my right stirrup and looked at India. I'd done it!

'One, two, three,' she counted. 'Four, five, six ...'

Slowly, the seconds ticked over.

Seven.

Eight.

Nine.

Lightning's body tensed.

Ten.

The girls joined India's chant.

Eleven.

Twelve.

I could feel Lightning tighten, like a huge ball. He danced on his feet, then reversed and spun around.

Fifteen.

'Go, girl!' someone yelled.

Lightning shied, then leaped into the air. I clung to his back, terror-struck. He landed on his forelegs and kicked out with his hind legs. I flew forward in the saddle and my face smashed into his neck. I felt something burst and my mouth filled with a gush of warmth. I spat and saw red.

The stallion kicked out again and again. I clung to the saddle and gripped with my legs as hard as I could. My muscles were burning. I crouched over and unpeeled my fingers from the pommel, reaching down to wrap my arms around his neck.

Twenty-three.

Twenty-four.

Lightning kicked out again. I felt his back legs go

up and up and up, like he was doing a handstand. I had nothing to hang on to and felt myself falling away from the saddle. I fought to stay on, fought with my hands, my legs, my whole body. But it wasn't enough. Just when I thought he'd tip right over, I was gone.

I smashed into his head on my way down, my stomach taking the brunt. I gasped and reached out with my hands. I could see grass and dirt. Then I crumpled hard against the earth.

I was lying on my face. I couldn't move. I couldn't breathe.

I heard a noise, like a pig squealing, and looked over my shoulder. All I could see was horse. His tummy gleamed like wet black rock, his forelegs thrashed. He held his head up high and screamed. I knew what was about to happen but couldn't do anything about it. Then there was crushing pain between my shoulders, as if something inside me had exploded. More pain, in my back, just above my waist. I prayed for it to be over, and then it was. No sound, no pain, just the rush of blood in my ears and the rasp of my own breathing.

I tried to get up. I couldn't move. I told my legs to work, to get me up and out of there, but nothing happened. I panicked and cried out loud. It sounded so far away.

I let my eyes close. It was over. India had won, but it didn't matter any more. Nothing mattered.

Then I felt hands on my head and feet. They slid something under me and clipped something cold around my neck. I opened my eyes and felt myself fly upwards for a moment, then something slammed into me and I was floating in white light.

A voice spoke to me. It was asking my name.

'Are you an angel?' I whispered.

I didn't know if they'd heard me, but they squeezed my hand and I felt safe.

There was a rocking motion. I didn't like it. I wanted that floaty feeling back. My stomach went into reverse and I threw up.

'There, now.' A lady's voice.

I tried to focus, to see who it was. She was beautiful with calm green eyes. She stroked my hair and I fell asleep. I don't remember anything else. No matter how many times I've been asked, I don't remember a single thing after that, not until I woke up.

The lights were bright and very white. There were people all around me talking fast and loudly. I was flat on my back with something strapped to my forehead. I'd never felt so much pain. I cried and asked for Mum, but there was a plastic mask over my nose and mouth and no one heard me. The mask was wet inside and made a hissing noise. I tried to rip it away but my hands wouldn't move. I tried to shake my head, to knock the mask off, but my head was stuck as well.

Someone asked me where the pain was and I said it was in my back and my neck. They talked even more then, but in a language I could barely understand, using words like 'CT scan' and 'MRI' and 'halo stabilization'.

'It hurts,' I sobbed.

A man who seemed impossibly tall told me I could have something for the pain in a little while, then turned to someone else and said I was 'lucid'.

I was so uncomfortable. I tried to wriggle, sure I would hurt less if I could just sit up or roll over or anything. But I couldn't move a single muscle. It was as if I was tied down to whatever I was lying on.

Someone picked up my arm and wiped the inside of my elbow with something cold. Then came a moment of terrible pain and I screamed. My arm was strapped with something like a ruler. I felt sticky stuff being wrapped around it and heard the rip of tape being pulled away from its dispenser.

The same tall man kept asking me over and over where it hurt and I told him. Then an army of people appeared and stood all around me and moved me onto another bed. They cut off my joddies, boots and T-shirt. It didn't take much to get my shirt off — it'd been slashed open by Lightning's shoes. I was embarrassed and cried. I didn't want to look at them so I closed my eyes, but a lady said I had to open them, and when I did she shone a light into them.

I blinked and wanted to rub my eyes but I couldn't move my hands. I started to scream again. I was angry and scared and hurting and all I wanted was my mum and to be able to move. I didn't know where I was or who I was with or what they were doing. I just wanted to go home. I screamed and screamed with my mouth wide open, and the tall man told me to stop but I couldn't. I tried to wrench my arms up and wriggled my legs and that was when someone picked up my hand again and counted.

'One, two, three …'

And then their voice faded to nothing and so did the pain.

twenty-two

Waking Up

When I woke up, I was frightened. I'd never been so frightened. I looked around me. There was no one else in the room, just machines that beeped and blinked. The walls were pale pink and there were animals painted on the window. There was a door, but it was glass. I was in some sort of cot with silver rails on each side. My hands ached, and when I tried to wriggle my fingers I felt something hard under them and realized they were bandaged. Then I remembered. I could see clear plastic tubes in my hands and felt one in my nose and at the back of my throat. I hated it. My mouth tasted awful, like I hadn't drunk anything in days. I tried to call out, but all I managed was a croak. I tried again and again, and finally managed a wail, like a wounded animal. It was a sound like nothing I'd ever heard and freaked me out even more.

The door opened and a nurse came in. Her hair was very short and coloured bright red and she had a gold ring in her nose. She smiled at me. 'Welcome back, sleepyhead.'

She patted my hair and did something to a plastic bag that hung from a silver stick beside my head.

'I'll get your parents and tell them the good news,' she said.

My heart leaped. Mum and Dad were here!

I wanted to talk to her but my voice refused to work. I croaked again and she offered me a cup with a bendy straw. I took a long drink and licked my lips. It was cool water. It tasted good, but my lips felt strange, all fat and broken and sore. I tried to touch them, but the movement tugged on the tube in my hand and hurt too much. I tried to sit up instead.

'No, you don't,' said the nurse.

She leaned forward and grabbed at a tube and pressed it and something went 'ding ding ding'. Almost at once there was another nurse there, and another. Then I heard someone crying and saying my name.

'Mum!'

It was the first proper word I'd managed, and then I cried as well.

Mum was at my side in a second. She kissed my face and my hand. 'We were so scared, Ash. We were so scared.' She said it over and over again.

'What happened to my mouth?' I asked.

Mum wiped at her teary face. 'You split your lips. Both of them. They've been stitched.'

'I just woke up and—'

I stopped. I didn't know what to say.

'Ash!'

It was Dad. I looked up at him. He was crying too. I'd never seen my father cry. Ever.

'Where's Jase?' I asked.

Dad blew his nose into a huge hanky. 'With Nan. We all came to stay here with her in town.'

'In town? What do you mean?' I felt so lost.

Dad explained that I'd been driven to the closest hospital to Linley, then flown to the city. Mrs Freeman had made the flight with me. I was in the Intensive Care Unit of the Children's Hospital and had been for two days. Jenna and her mum had come to see me, but I'd been given stuff to make me sleep and keep me still.

I was shocked. I couldn't believe I'd been unconscious for so long.

'I'll call Jenna soon and tell her you're awake,' Dad said. He looked so tired. 'That you're okay.'

'Why did they want to keep me still?' I asked, and looked into his eyes. I trusted Dad. He was the best nurse Shady Creek had ever seen and the best dad in the whole world. He'd tell me the truth. He'd know how to fix me. 'Am I okay?'

I waited for him to smile and say I was fine and I'd be riding Honey in no time and that everything would be all right. But he didn't.

'You've been through testing and the doctors are doing everything they can. But they don't know for sure.'

'Don't know what?' I was terrified. I tried to wriggle my toes. I couldn't tell if they obeyed me or not.

'They don't know if your back's okay. They think you might have fractured your spine.'

'But they can make it better, right?' I said. I licked my lips. They were sharp and dry. I tried to think positive, but deep down, in the pit of my soul, something was gnawing at me. I needed my back to walk. I needed it to do a lot of things. 'When can I ride again? I need to get back to polocrosse training. Our first competition match is … Dad?'

Dad had looked away from me and was staring at his hands. Something was wrong. Something was very, very wrong.

'They don't know if you'll be able to ride again,' he said.

'What?'

I couldn't believe it. He was joking. He had to be joking. This was all a dream and I'd wake up and be at Linley, torturing the violin and doing my Geography skills test and hiding from Mrs Wright and everything would be the same.

'No!' I cried.

'It's okay, possum,' Mum said, holding my hand.

I couldn't speak. I just sobbed.

I couldn't live if I couldn't ride. I was Ashleigh Louise Miller, horse rider. Without riding I was nothing. I was a no one. I may as well not even exist.

'Give it time, Ash,' Dad said, tears running down his face. 'You never know. They're being cautious. It's always the way with spinal injuries.'

'I wanna go home,' I said.

'Soon,' Mum said, trying to soothe me. 'Soon, possum.'

Nothing they said or did could comfort me. I sobbed and sobbed, even when the doctor came to see me, while he read the papers that hung from the end of my bed and pointed at X-rays and talked about acute trauma evaluation. What if it was true? What if I could never ride again? What if I couldn't even walk? What would happen then?

The doctor left at last. I was tired, so tired. I closed my eyes again. I felt Mum's arm around me, felt her breathing near me, and fell asleep.

When I woke up again it was dark. I'd always hated waking up in darkness, knowing I'd slept the day away.

'Good to see you,' a voice said.

I looked up. 'Jenna?' I could speak better now at least. But my mouth still tasted awful. I would have given anything for a toothbrush.

'The one and only,' she replied.

I began to cry. I hadn't seen her for so long and I'd missed her so much. Now we were together again and I was flat on my back with tubes sticking in and out of me, feeling sore and scared and sorry.

'What's happened to me?' I said.

Jenna looked around, then got up and closed the door quietly. 'Your spine isn't fractured,' she told me. 'They found out a little while ago. But it's badly bruised and something in there's swollen with some fluid. That horse stomped on you, Ash. On purpose.'

I gasped. 'That's impossible.'

Jenna shook her head and held out my drink. I sipped gratefully. 'It's true,' she said. 'One of those horrible girls recorded the whole thing on her phone. The doctors saw what happened, so did your mum and dad. It totally freaked them out.'

'Where are they?'

'Mum took them home for dinner. They haven't eaten since they got the call from Linley Heights.'

Jenna told me the rest of the story: how Linley Heights had exploded; how there'd been an inquiry and every single girl who'd attended the challenge had been interviewed, including Ricki. She'd been the one who ran for help. By the time the ambulance arrived, I'd been lying in that paddock for an hour. The anti-horse committee had got hold of the footage and President Carlson was holding an emergency Parents' Association meeting. India McCray had been suspended until next term.

I didn't feel any delight at knowing India had got what she deserved. All I could think of was that the horses would go. And it'd be all my fault.

I lay there for a while, stewing. Tears ran down my face but my hands hurt so much I couldn't wipe them away. My nose ran and my mouth still tasted terrible and my back was so sore!

Then I found myself telling Jenna everything. About the challenge and India and Claire. About how Em had been banned from being anywhere near me. About how Becky had frozen me out and how scared I was about what had happened to me. About what could still happen to me. She listened and held my hand and wiped at my face with a tissue every now and then.

'My back hurts,' I moaned eventually. 'I need the nurse.'

Jenna's face lit up. 'You can feel it hurting? Where?'

'Don't be so happy about it,' I groaned.

'Don't you get it? You can feel.' Jenna's eyes were bright.

I held her hand and we waited together for the nurse. I'd never been so glad to see her. We'd been torn apart and been through more than I could say. But we were still best friends and I was so proud of that.

The nurse came and put something into one of

the tubes and I fell asleep again, my hand warm inside Jenna's. I dreamed for the first time since the accident. I dreamed of horses and hitting the ground and pain and trying to cry out for help. I dreamed of Lightning's feet and legs thrashing above me and the glint of sunlight on his shoes. I heard the sound of my bones being crushed and woke up alone, sweating and breathing fast.

I told myself it was only a dream. Nothing to be scared of. I was safe now and they were making me better. But the fear kept pounding inside my chest like a heartbeat. All that night I saw Lightning's hooves over and over. I could taste the fear in my mouth and felt the blood burst from my nose. I heard the stallion's scream and felt again and again the sickening thud of my body crumpling against the earth.

My heart beat hard. Sweat pooled under my arms and on my chest. I gasped for breath. I'd never known anything like this. Not ever. By morning it had all but consumed me.

I would never ride again.

Not because I couldn't, but because I was too scared to.

twenty-three

Big Decisions

'Ow, ow, ow!' Jason babbled up at me.

'You're telling me,' I grouched. Jason held on to a chair, wobbling on his fat baby legs. His hair was starting to curl into fine dark rings. 'Very, very ow!'

Mum gazed at Jason. 'Isn't he cute? Just the cutest, most gorgeous gorgeous!'

'I'm the one at death's door here,' I said, rolling my eyes. 'Would it be too much to ask for a little attention?'

I was still flat on my back, but unstrapped now and feeling a little better. It was day four, and my hair had been washed and had the knots brushed out of it and I'd had a bath — a wash, anyway. I'd started some gentle physiotherapy with a doctor

302

who'd moved my legs and arms around for a while, and even moved my neck. Flowers and goodies had been pouring into my room all morning and my little brother had come to see me. What more could a girl want?

Just one thing. For the doctors to march in through that door and tell me to get up off this bed and go home!

'Are you in pain?' Mum asked.

'Of course,' I snapped. 'I was crushed by a horse, remember?'

As I heard myself I winced. After everything I'd put Mum through, I was giving her attitude. I just couldn't help it. It was all bubbling up inside me and I wasn't strong enough to push it back down.

'This sucks,' I said. 'I am *so* bored.'

Mum sighed. 'I'm afraid you'll have to put up with it. Bed rest, physio and painkillers are about the best they can do for you.'

'For how long?' I said. I wanted to scream. I wanted to rip the bed apart.

'For as long as it takes the swelling to go down. You should be thanking your lucky horseshoes you got away with just swelling. It could have been much worse.'

I rolled my eyes. 'Whatever. As long as I can walk, that's all I want. Which reminds me — I want you to get rid of all my riding stuff before I get home. I don't want it. I don't wanna even look at it.'

'What are you talking about?' Mum stared at me as if I'd turned into someone she didn't know.

'I mean it,' I said. 'Please, just clear it all out. I don't need it any more.'

'You've had a fall, Ash. It happens. There's no need to undo your life.'

'Listen to me,' I cried. 'I hate riding. I'm never riding again!'

'Are you sure about this?' Mum said, her eyes serious.

'Of course I'm sure. I don't care what you do with it. Sell it. Give it away.' I squeezed my eyes shut to stop the tears.

'What about Honey?' Mum's voice was soft.

I opened and closed my mouth but no words came out. I hadn't thought about Honey. Did giving away riding mean giving her away as well? I supposed it did. But would I be able to live without her? No way.

'Maybe she can stay at Linley,' I said slowly. 'They need good school horses.'

'You don't mean that.' Mum held out her hands to Jason and he took a shaky step towards her then fell flat on his backside. 'Good thing that nappy gives him plenty of padding.'

'Yeah,' I said. 'You don't want two of us on your hands, do you?'

Mum gave me a look. 'I must ask the doctor next time she comes to see you if that stuff they're giving you to kill your pain is also killing your manners.'

'Send Honey to live with Becky,' I said. 'Or better still, with Mrs Mac.'

'Enough!' Mum cried. 'You're delirious. Besides, you still have Toffee. Who's gonna want a maniac miniature pony? You know he's gone through three new soccer balls since you left for boarding school. Found his way into Flea's place too. Terrorized that rotten nag of his — what's his name? Scrub?'

'Scud.' I grimaced. 'Another psycho horse. Suits Flea to the bottom of his riding boots.'

'That's the one. By the time we found Toff, Scud was quivering in the corner of his paddock. Like an elephant scared of a mouse.' She grinned at Jason again. 'Look at my big boy! Crawling to his mummy.'

'His knees are black,' I said. 'The floor's prob'ly covered with germs.' I couldn't believe I'd said that.

I'd spent too much time with Claire Carlson. I was becoming her! I shook my head.

'Don't do that!' Mum yelped. 'Keep still. It's only for a few weeks. Better to stay still for a few weeks and walk away, than act crazy and wind up in rehab.'

I gritted my teeth. She was making sense, I knew it. But I was feeling crazy. I'd never done so little in my life. I was always up to my elbows in something — grooming, riding, feeding, mucking out, training. But all that was behind me now. I had to think still thoughts. Imagine I was a telegraph pole, a street sign, a statue. I couldn't stand it.

Jason pulled himself up using Mum's leg for support. Then he stood tall, let go and wobbled towards my bed, laughing. His bottom teeth stuck out and his chin ran with dribble.

'Did you see that, Ash? Did you? He walked. He took his first steps.' Mum picked Jase up and held him in her arms, dancing and kissing his fat cheeks again and again. 'What a shame Dad missed out. He missed your first steps too.'

'Keep hold of him 'til Dad gets back,' I said. 'He can save up his next first steps.'

Mum sighed and cuddled Jason close. 'It's a huge deal, quitting riding.'

'Look at me,' I said, and stared up at the ceiling, praying to the horse … No, I couldn't pray to them any more. They'd done nothing to save me in that paddock. 'What else can I do?' I finished.

'But it's all you've ever wanted. You're a born horseperson. Your first word was "pony"!'

Anger surged through me. Mum had spent half my life trying to talk me out of horses and the other half complaining about how much it all cost.

'D'you want me dead or something?' I snapped.

'Ashleigh! How could you say such a thing?' Mum looked as though she couldn't decide between being really hurt or really mad.

I refused to answer her. I didn't want to look at her either, but I couldn't storm out of the room, or roll over and bury my face in the pillow, or even reach for a pair of sunglasses. So I just closed my eyes.

'As soon as you're up and about, you're grounded,' Mum said.

She threw herself into a chair, Jason curled up on her lap, and stared out of the window. It would've been nice to do the same. She was right: I was a horseperson. But although I loved, lived, breathed and dreamed horses, I was also afraid of riding now.

Lightning had crushed more than my bones with his thrashing hooves. He'd crushed my spirit too.

'You know, sometimes I just don't understand you,' Mum said at last. 'We were worried out of our minds. What on earth possessed you to try to ride a wild horse?'

I stared up at the ceiling. I'd been doing a whole lot of that the last few days. I made a mental note to write a strongly worded letter to the hospital manager. Surely patients in traction would recover more quickly if they had something interesting to look at.

My head was choked with thoughts, so many thoughts that it started to ache. There were questions that only I could answer. Why had I accepted India's dumb challenge? Why had I even cared what she thought? Why had I cared what anyone thought? I realized then and there that I didn't have to prove myself to anyone any more. I had never had to in the first place. The only person's approval that I needed was my own.

My eyes filled with tears that stung. I didn't want to be here, in this rotten bed. All I wanted now was a second chance. A chance to get better, to start again at Linley. It hadn't been worth it. Nothing could ever be worth this.

'Talk to me!' Mum said, standing up suddenly and balancing Jason on her hip. He grabbed a handful of her shirt and shoved it into his mouth.

I shook my head. The tears were making it impossible to speak.

'Ash.' Mum's voice was softer now. She sighed. 'It's okay, possum. I guess you'll talk when you're ready.'

She paused, and I could tell she was biting her bottom lip. I do that too. I suppose I get it from her.

'I don't know how to say this,' she went on, 'so I'll just come out with it. Dad and I have talked and we feel it's best to bring you home.'

I cleared my throat. 'I was hoping you'd say that. I don't wanna spend the rest of my life staring at that crack.' I pointed at the ceiling.

'I don't think you're getting me,' Mum said. 'We want to bring you home from Linley. For good.'

I looked at her properly for the first time that afternoon. 'What?'

'We weren't sure, but then you said you wanted to give riding away and that helped me make up my mind.' Mum patted Jason's back and he rested his head on her shoulder and stuck his fingers in his mouth.

'How could you decide something like this without even asking me what I think?' I said. I couldn't believe what I was hearing. Okay, so I might have said I didn't want to ride any more. But I'd never said I wanted to leave Linley.

'We're your parents. I think that gives us the right to make a decision every once in a while,' Mum snapped. 'Honestly, Ash. What if something really terrible had happened to you? What if that horse had stomped on you harder or higher? Do you really understand what we'd be dealing with right now? Do you?'

I glared at the ceiling, choking back tears. Of course I understood.

'I need a break,' Mum said. 'And Jason needs his nappy changed.'

She grabbed her bag and promised to be back soon.

I lay there and thought about life without Linley. It meant no more Claire and India and Mrs Wright. It meant no more violin and Latin. No more fishcakes for lunch, or fighting over the TV or having to share a room. But it also meant life without Ricki and Em and Maryanne James. And even though I'd decided I'd never ride again, I'd miss the excitement of polocrosse matches and living amongst the horse crazy. If I left Linley, I'd always wonder what might have been.

But could I stay at Linley and not ride? I was there on a scholarship so wouldn't they expect me to ride? And how would Mum and Dad afford the fees and everything else without my scholarship? Maybe that was part of the reason they wanted to take me away from Linley, because they didn't have enough money.

I thought about what it would be like going to Shady Creek and Districts High School instead. No one would expect anything of me there. I could be with Pree and Becky and no one would think any less of me for surviving Lightning and giving up horses. Becky and Pree may never forgive me for giving up horses. But I was sure at least that Pree would understand.

Tears rose in my eyes again as I thought about Becky. Ricki and Em had called every hour until I'd woken up, then at least three times a day after that. But Becky hadn't called or sent a message with Mum and Dad. Had she heard about my accident? Or did she just not care? Maybe she wouldn't want me to go to school with her.

There were so many questions clogging up my mind. And not an answer in sight.

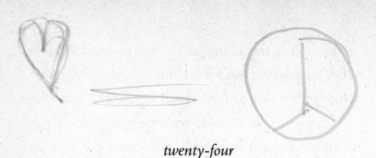

twenty-four

Pros and Cons

I couldn't believe I was home at last. Three weeks I'd spent in that bed in the Children's Hospital. They'd wanted to keep me in another week, but Dad's assurances that nothing but the best of his professional care would be available to me twenty-four hours a day and that he had contacts galore at Shady Creek and Districts Hospital had softened them. I was as stiff as an old pair of reins, but at least my back didn't hurt. I was actually allowed to be in a semi-sitting up position which, after lying as flat as a cane toad on a Queensland highway, was nothing less than delicious.

'So how does it feel to be back in your own room?'

Dad beamed at me from the doorway. He'd spent days fixing the place up as some kind of invalid recovery resort, even breaking his very own Number One Golden Rule by setting up a TV on my desk!

'Good,' I said. 'Great! Even though I'm still lying down, with my very own remote control I feel like queen of the house!'

Dad glowered. 'Don't get used to it, Your Highness.'

I held up my hands. 'I know, I know. The traditional owner of the remote control is the dad. Randomly selecting channels every four seconds reminds him of his origins as a hunter and makes him feel—'

Dad made a choking noise. 'Where on earth did you learn that?'

I grinned. 'TV.'

He rolled his eyes. 'You have some visitors. Shall I let them in, or are you still too delicate?'

My heart flip-flopped. 'Who is it?'

'Becky and Pree.' Dad raised his eyebrows. 'I believe they've brought gifts as well as themselves.'

'Dad!' I wailed.

'Well?'

I stared at the ceiling. Another ceiling, but at least it was all my very own. 'Send 'em in,' I said finally.

Dad smiled and gave me the thumbs up. 'Adda girl.'

He left me and closed the door. I lay in bed, still sore and still afraid. So very, very afraid. Afraid of riding, afraid of going back to Linley, afraid of not going back. And right at that moment, I was really afraid of seeing Becky and Pree. Would Becky be my friend again or would she still be weird, like last time?

There was a knock on my door.

'Come in,' I called. My voice gave nothing away of the turmoil inside me.

The door opened and a familiar face peeked inside.

'Ash!' it said.

'Pree!'

Priyanka Prasad bounded across the room and wrapped her arms around my neck, then jumped away suddenly. 'Oh no! I shouldn't have done that. Dad gave me this big lecture about not hurting your back and here I go treating you like origami. Sorry, Ash! Hey, have you heard this one? Why couldn't the pony sing well? Coz his voice was a little hoarse!'

'Good one,' I said. 'Where's Becky?'

Pree wrinkled her nose. 'Becks? Where are you hiding?'

Becky stepped into the room, an awkward smile on her face. Her long black hair hung straight down like a sheet of silk. I beamed when I saw her.

'Hi,' she said, and stared at the floor.

My heart sank like a bit in a barrel of water. She was still being weird.

'How are you, you know, feeling?' She toyed with the door handle.

I shifted a little in bed. 'Good. Better. Thanks.'

Becky took another step inside, then another. 'I was really freaked out when Mum told me what happened. I never thought any of us'd ever be hurt like that. They flew you to hospital in a *helicopter*!'

I nodded. 'I know. Don't remember a thing, though.'

'It was your first flight and you slept right through it!' Becky laughed. 'Typical of you, Ash!'

And I knew my friend was back. For now, anyway.

Becky and Pree handed over a present they'd gone in for together. I tore away the wrapping. It was a big, beautiful book about rodeo riding.

'To add to your collection,' Becky said.

'We figured you'd already made a start on that stallion.' Pree winked.

'You could have a big career ahead of you,' Becky added, grinning.

'Funny,' I said.

I opened the book. There was an inscription: *To Ashleigh, Our best friend. Get well soon, love always from Becky and Pree.*

'Thanks, guys.'

I didn't know what else to say. It was so good to be with them, to have things back to normal.

'Hey guys, have you heard this one?' Pree said. 'Why was the rodeo horse rich?'

'Because he had a lot of bucks!' Becky and I cried together.

Pree was amazed. 'Have I told you that one before?'

Becky and I burst out laughing.

Pree's dad arrived early to pick her up and then it was just me and Becky. The way it had always been. We lay on my bed, leaning up against each other, watching TV. She'd brought a bag of prawn chips for me and I shoved them into my mouth one after the other. Not easy on your back, but definitely worth it.

'So why?' I said eventually. I didn't want to upset her, but I had to know. 'Why'd you freeze me out that time?'

Becky shrugged. 'I'm an idiot.'

'No, you're not.' I took another prawn chip and chewed thoughtfully. 'But I really do wanna know. Did I do something wrong?'

'You didn't do anything wrong.' Becky sighed and grabbed the remote. She flicked through the stations, settling on a show about frogs. 'How long are they gonna let you keep this in here? It's brilliant.'

'Until I'm better. And don't change the subject.'

Becky sighed again and flicked the TV off. A strange peace descended on the room.

'I thought you'd forget about me,' she said. 'I thought you'd come back all full of Linley and I was scared. I wanted to protect myself. I dunno, I just get like that sometimes. It's not easy to be ... to be ...'

I held her hand. 'I know, Beck.'

I didn't need her to say anything more. I didn't even want her to. She had never stopped being my friend. I had learned a few things since my accident; all that time I'd spent staring at the ceiling. It had started with those questions I'd had to ask myself

317

and ended with answers I never expected. The best thing about those answers was that every single one of them had come from somewhere inside of me. I'd learned that friends are precious. You can never have too many and you have to treat them well. A bit like horses, really.

Long after Becky had gone home and I'd watched so much TV my eyes were aching, I switched it off and sort of rolled out of bed. The physiotherapist at the hospital had made me promise to exercise and there was a little bloke outside I needed to see. I had the feeling he could help me out with a problem I was having.

I took the stairs slowly with Mum's help, every step ripping at the muscles in my back, until finally I was in the kitchen, then at the back door, then at the bottom of the steps. Then, after a rest, I was in the paddock. Mum ran back inside to check on Jason and I was alone.

The paddock was so empty without Honey. My gorgeous girl was still at Linley. I hadn't seen her since the day of the accident and I missed her.

I leaned back against the fence and breathed in as deeply as I could. Home. Horses. Wet grass and dirt and hay and chaff and horses and poo and horses. Did I really want to give all this up?

And what about school? I could stay here, go to SCD High and things would be the same as they'd always been. Except for the riding. Or I could fuss and wail and carry on until Mum and Dad took me back to Linley. Where I'd no longer have a scholarship, take Horsemanship classes or play polocrosse. Where everybody was always watching you. Where you had to get yourself out of bed in the morning, and make sure your schoolbooks were packed before you went to bed at night. Where you had to draw an imaginary line down the middle of the room and try to stop your sludge from creeping across. Where everything was exciting and amazing and wonderful and terrible all at once.

I felt something warm and prickly and wet in my hand and looked down and there he was.

'Toffee!' I cried. 'My main man.'

I'd only seen my miniature pony from my bedroom window since I'd got home. With Honey still at Linley, he was my only equine friend.

'Whaddya think, Toff?' I said, rubbing under his forelock. 'What should I do?'

'Has he got any insights?'

I clutched my chest. 'Dad! You scared me.'

Dad grinned and shrugged. 'Sorry.'

I smiled up at him and tugged gently on Toffee's ear. It was smooth on one side, fuzzy on the other. A bit like life, really.

'How are you feeling? About leaving Linley?' Dad tousled my hair then leaned against the fence next to me.

'You promised you'd stop doing that once I started high school!' I said, smoothing my hair down again. I hoped that Flea was off being a Creepketeer with Carly and Ryan and nowhere near tousle central.

Dad laughed aloud. 'Never! You'll always be my little girl, Ash. Always and always.'

'Dad?' I leaned into his chest.

'Uh-huh?'

'I'm not sure I wanna leave Linley. But I'm scared to go back.'

Dad wrapped his arms around me and I snuggled in, not caring one bit if Flea saw me. 'Sounds like you've got some thinking to do, kiddo.'

'You're telling me. Trouble is, I dunno where to start. My head gets too full of thoughts and I just give up.'

'Make a list.'

I pushed away and stared up into his face. 'Huh?'

'Whenever I'm in a real pickle—'

'Dad, *no one* says they're in a pickle these days. Even if they are. You are *so* old-fashioned!'

Dad rubbed at his chin, thinker-style. 'Okay. Whenever I'm trying to make a decision that seems impossible, I write a list of pros and cons. The pros are the good things and the cons are the bad things. If the pros outweigh the cons, then I—'

'Go with the pros.' I sighed. 'But what if there are heaps and heaps of cons.'

'I guess I'd have to decide against whatever it was I wanted to do. Unless I wanted it so much the cons just didn't matter.'

I wrinkled my nose. 'D'you really do the list for real?'

Dad nodded. 'You bet. Like when we were trying to decide whether or not to move to Shady Creek, and whether or not to open Miller Lodge.' He smiled. 'And whether or not to rent out your room.'

'Dad!' I pretend-whacked him.

'I'll take that as my cue to leave,' he said, tousling my hair.

This time I didn't smooth it down. I knew it meant he loved me.

I did write that list. Late that night, when everyone in the house was sleeping. I drew back my curtains and sat at my desk, watching Toffee in the paddock and writing, and ended up with a list where one column was much longer than the other.

My decision was easy. Convincing Mum and Dad to let me go back to Linley Heights School would be the complete opposite.

twenty-five

Back to School

'How are you feeling? Can I get you anything? Are you hungry? Thirst—'

'Mum!' I wailed. I was sitting cross-legged on my bed. It was so good to be sitting. I never wanted to lie down again. 'You're killing me!'

'Don't say that!' Mum held her hands over her ears. 'I don't want to hear those words come out of your mouth ever again.'

'Puh-lease,' I groaned. 'But seriously, nothing will ever kill me again.' I patted her knee brightly.

'Ash!' Mum cried, frantically tapping her fingers on my bedhead. 'Touch wood, touch wood!'

'Mum, listen!' The news I had for her was way

so much more important than her newly found superstitions. 'I got an email from Ricki.'

Mum's tapping stopped. 'Today's technology will never cease to amaze me.'

I was buzzing, fizzing, electrified! 'She says the Board has voted for the riding program. They figured they'd lose too many students and Linley could never survive without it!'

Mum smiled. 'There you go.'

'And she said they said something about tradition and Linley's uniqueness and a whole heap of really amazing people have come from Linley and—'

'So you'll—'

'And even that cellphone footage of my accident didn't stop them and guess what else?' I grabbed her hand and squeezed it.

'What?' she said softly.

'Em's allowed to be a vet if she wants!' I threw my head back and laughed. 'It's so unreal, I mean, her mum and dad said that as long as she's some kind of doctor they'll be okay with it. She must have really stood up to them. Can you believe it?'

Mum shook her head.

I beamed. 'Unbelievable!'

Mum let go of my hand and looked down at the bed. She picked a little at some fuzz and sighed.

'What is it, Mum?' I said, my excitement wearing off quickly.

She smiled weakly at me. 'I was kinda hoping you, that you'd … oh, I don't know.'

I looked into her eyes intently. 'That I'd what?'

She took my hand, running her fingers gently over mine. 'I'm your mum and I want you to be happy and have everything you want. Maybe it's selfish of me. But I was kind of hoping you'd want to stay here with us.' Mum smiled and shook her head. 'Thing is, I know you, Ash. You can say all you want about not riding, but I know you'll miss Linley. And I know you'll ride again some day.'

I shook my head. 'I don't know if I can, Mum. I don't know if I'm brave like Em or cool like Ricki.'

'So you'll stay?' Mum said, brightening. 'Help us in the B and B. I'd rather have you making the beds than lying in them.'

'That isn't funny.' I gave her a sour look. It was hard enough, what with everything that was going on in my head about horses and riding and wondering whether or not I would ever know that in-the-saddle feeling again, without Mum cracking bad jokes. I realized something for sure in that moment. I wanted to feel weightless again. I wanted to feel like I could fly. I wanted to feel that Honey and I were one being, with one mind and one heart that beat along with her hooves. Yes, I really wanted to ride.

Mum sighed again. 'I only want to take care of you. You're my baby.'

'I'm twelve,' I said, reaching for my Latin book. I had so much work to catch up on.

'Twelve, a hundred and twelve — what do I care? You'll always be my baby.' Mum smiled at me and sat at the foot of my bed. 'Give your poor old mum a break. I'll only get to see you twelve weeks and a few exeat weekends a year from now until you're eighteen. Let me enjoy you while you're here.'

I gave her a look. 'Does this mean I can go back to Linley?'

Mum sighed. 'I've thought about it. A lot. And your dad and I have talked and talked and talked.'

'And?'

I was so hopeful. I'd given them such a fright. Let's face it, I'd given myself a fright. I still didn't know if I'd ever be able to get back on a horse, but I had to try. And Linley Heights was the best place for me to do it.

'We think you should go.' Mum's voice was small.

I smiled. 'Are you sure?'

'No,' Mum said. She picked up the Latin book, now abandoned at my feet, and turned over the first few pages. 'But we don't see any point in withdrawing you. You'll have opportunities at Linley we never had. With or without the riding.'

'But …' I swallowed. It was hard to pull one of my deepest fears from the pit of my stomach and spit it out. 'But what if they … what if they take my scholarship away?'

Mum shrugged. 'They might. But they might not. Either way, we'll manage.'

I threw my arms around her neck and held her close. Mum held me tight.

'I'd better make the most of these,' she said, laughing.

I pulled back. 'The most of what?'

'These cuddles! One day you might decide you're way too big and mature to cuddle your mum.' She tucked a wisp of hair behind my ear and stroked my face.

'I hope not!' I said. I couldn't imagine it for a minute.

Mum held out her arms. 'I hope not too!'

I sat there on my bed long after she'd gone downstairs. I was going back to Linley! There were so many challenges to meet, so many questions to answer. I pulled a piece of paper from the top drawer of my desk and started to make another list. But this time it wasn't pros and cons. It was all the things I wanted to do with my second chance — at life and at Linley.

Give up violin, learn to play bassoon.

Get a hundred per cent in History and put a smile on Mrs Wright's face rather than wipe it off.

Give Honey a hundred thousand million kisses and at least three bags of carrots.

See if Lightning's okay.

Thank Mrs Freeman.

Rub Claire Carlson's face in horse poo.

Get back on a horse.

And that was only for starters.

Glossary

agisted boarded

bathers swimsuit

bindi-eye weed-like plant known for its sharp-needled seeds

blub short for 'blubber': to cry

boot the trunk of a car

chaff mix of hay and straw fed to horses

dunny toilet

exeat weekend long weekend

float horse trailer; to transport a horse by trailer

fringe bangs

gymkhana an equestrian event, usually for young people, that involves timed games for riders on horses

a heap, heaps a lot, lots

joddies abbreviation for jodhpurs

kindy abbreviation for kindergarten

mahooky trouble

nag an old or worn-out horse

nappy diaper

Old Girl a graduate (of Linley Heights)

polocrosse a combination of polo and lacrosse

ring to call on the telephone

ruck a loose scrum (as in rugby)

strangles an infectious disease in horses that causes inflamed nasal passages and abscesses around the throat

titbit tidbit

uni abbreviation for university

ute a pickup truck; abbreviation for utility vehicle

Acknowledgements

I would like to thank my publisher at HarperCollins, Lisa Berryman, and my editors, Lydia Papandrea and Nicola O'Shea, for their guidance, encouragement and incredible work in helping to make *Horse Mad Heights* a reality. To my beautiful kids, Mariana, John and Simon — I love you. You make my world an amazing place. To my husband, Seb, life is magical because of you. And to the readers of the series, thank you for your emails, your letters and your horse madness!

Photo by Dyan Hallworth

KATHY HELIDONIOTIS lives in Sydney and divides her time between writing stories, reading good books, teaching and looking after her three gorgeous children. Kathy has had thirteen children's books published so far. *Horse Mad Heights* is the sixth book in the popular Horse Mad series.

Visit Kathy at her website:
www.kathyhelidoniotis.com

In the same series

Totally Horse Mad

Horse Mad Summer

Horse Mad Academy

Horse Mad Heroes

Horse Mad Western